David Toulmin
Harvest Home

Pan Books London and Sydney

All the characters in this book are fictitious
and any resemblance to actual persons,
living or dead, is purely coincidental

First published 1978 by Paul Harris Publishing Edinburgh
This edition published 1980 by Pan Books Ltd,
Cavaye Place, London SW10 9PG
© David Toulmin 1977
ISBN 0 330 25938 5
Made and printed in Great Britain by
C. Nicholls & Company Ltd, Philips Park Press, Manchester

To Ann Strachan, Lorna Morrison and Beryl Stott,
the three quines who married our loons,
this beuk is a dedication

Mull o' Rora's fite futret ran roon aboot
Mull o' Rora's rollers and Mull o' Rora's rollers
Ran roon aboot!

Contents

Harvest Home

Jonathan McGillivray had been the blacksmith at Bourie for as long as most folk could mind, and he had shod their horses and metalled their ploughs and rung their cart wheels since some of the fairmer cheils were in hippens, comin' on for forty year maybe and nae much change in the man: a bit crook in his back from leaning over horses' hoofs with a burning shoe, held with a spike in his hand, his fingers gnarled into the curve of the hammer handle, his old bald head polished like a yellow turnip for the spring show, but as swack as ever at the picnic races and still as fond o' a dram. An gin there was a concert in the Bourie Hall he could give you a tune on the fiddle, skreichin' awa' up there on the stage, his red face like a full moon newly risen at the end o' hairst, and again you would find the blacksmith at the Meal and Ale celebrations.

But Jonathan McGillivray was a name far too long for the farming cheils in the Bogside, especially in the hairst time when they were hurried, so they just called him Jotty, and Jotty it had been for some of them since they were toddlers. So the hairst comin' on folk began to look out their binder canvasses that were mostly kept on the rafters of the corn loft, away from the vermin, and they would take them to the saddler for repair, maybe a bit stick to tack on here and there and some patching to do and buckles to be sewn on; and besides his harness duties the saddler was fair stacked up with wark, so that he had to send some of the binder canvasses to the sail-maker down at the harbour in the toon. The farmer billies had forgotten all about their canvasses in the height of summer, when the saddler was slack, and now they all came jing-bang, in the mou' o' hairst, and there was a great clamour for repairs at the last minute. Others had forgotten to order binder-twine and the agents' lugs were ringing with the dirl of the telephone, which was something new in the Bogside.

Some folk had to take their binders to the smiddy for mechanical repair and there was another hue-and-cry for spare bits. There were the few who were methodical and had things done on time, but most of the farming cheils were easy going and left everything until the last minute; and maybe you couldn't blame them when you thought of the patience they had to have with the weather, waiting an opportunity to handle their crops, long over-ripe and rotting in the process. Nature was their schoolmistress and she had taught them patience from the day of their birth, snatching at her skirts but wary of her moods, awaiting her smiles and the shake of her apron, when they could gather in plenty from the sunny fields. It was an environment that would have sent the factory-bred boardroom mind to the wall; and maybe it accounted for the tolerant attitude of the farming cheils, 'glad of small mercies' as they say, the children of a mistress whose tears are slow in drying. Some of them will tell you that the weather clerk is boss and the banker is the farmer; that they themselves are only caretakers looking after the place and the most they can hope for is to die in debt.

The factory chiefs have only strikes to contend with but the farmers have Mother Nature, and when she weeps over the harvest fields her tears are a desolation. In 1927 she had a fit of weeping, the likes of which their fathers had never seen before, nor their children since. In fact the farmers thought she had pished herself and when the sun appeared they said he was only out for a wee-wee. Sometimes he came out on stilts to keep his feet dry, staring down those shafts of light piercing the storm clouds the sunscape artists love to paint but are hated by the farmers. Almost every day there was a 'tooth' in the sky, mostly on the sea, the broken pillar of a rainbow, the other end of it shining in somebody's park of wet stooks, with a bit missing overhead, and this phenomenon appeared so very often that folk began to talk of the Rainbow Hairst, and whether it was at even or morning it was always a warning to the farming billies that the umbrella sky was leaking.

'Sic seed sic leed' they used to say, meaning that the harvest would be as the seed time had been, yet the spring of that year had been a moderate one, so the farmers never trusted Dame Nature after that. Most of them had barometers on their lobby walls and when they tapped them in the mornings they nearly fell off the hooks, always at rain and still falling, while outside in the close the hens refused to take shelter and the cats in the steading washed over their lugs, sure signs of rain, while old men complained of rheumatism and stinging corns. Over the parks the oyster-catcher birds were skirling for more and still more of Mother Nature's tears. There were even jokes about it; like the loon who said to himself 'The mair rain the mair rest,' hoping to get a sleep in the straw, but when the farmer overheard him he changed it to 'The mair rain the mair girse (grass)' and the farmer forgave him.

Our farmer cheils are the unspoilt sons of Mother Nature and in 1927 she threw the book at them: rain hail sleet snow and thunder; frost that turned their turnips to stone, and when they burned their useless crops she sent gales to fan the roaring flames across the corn fields, the night skies red with conflagration. That which was too sodden to burn went under the plough and the spring of the following year was a paradise. It seemed that Mother Nature relented for her sons and she gave them a harvest that lasted only a month, but with a slightly lower yield than most.

But when the farmers brought their binders to Jotty the black-smith he dirled his hammer on the ringing anvil and said: 'Dammit tae hell, couldn't ye have come sooner!' thinking that experience would have taught them better over the years, though it never did, and they never listened to his advice or admonishment. Now as always in late summer Jotty was surrounded with binders, so that folk with their motor cars could hardly get by on the road: what with Deering, Albion, McCormick, Massey-Harris, Hornsby, Sunshine, Milwaukie, Wallace (Frost & Wood), Osborne, Bisset etc, all the popular makes, and all waiting for spare parts from the makers, delivered by bus or carrier from the agents in Aberdeen, like Barclay Ross & Tough (later Barclay Ross & Hutchison), or Reid & Leys, or even from as far afield as George Sellar & Son Ltd in Huntly, more famous for their ploughs than binder spare parts. Jotty's wife poor soul was up to the eyes in invoices and accounts, with hardly time to tidy up her house or cook a decent diet for her man and his assistant. What with the usual wark of shoeing horses and his ain crop to harvest, though it was only a few acres, Jotty had his sleeves rolled up to his arse 'ole almost, all day and half the night, with hardly time to fill his pipe, smoking more spunks than tobacco, and for want of nicotine he was short tempered and ready to snap your nose off as soon as you put it round the top half of the door that was always open in daytime.

On Monday mornings Jotty would tell you he had worked all day on Sunday while you was sitting sleeping in the kirk, and that the minister worked only one day a week while he worked seven; unless there was a wedding or a funeral, or even a christening, which wasn't all that often in the Bogside, and you said it wasn't all that wonder then that some blacksmiths had gone in for the clergy and turned their collars back to front. But this only angered Jotty worse and he refused to shoe the shelt you had brought with you, riding on its back to the smiddy. 'Dammit tae hell,' says he, his fusker sticking out like a byre broom – 'it's juist sae muckle a body can do!' So you had to threaten to take the shelt away again before he would shoe it, and he was a bit feared to let you do that, lest he offend the farmer cheil you worked for; so you just had to be prepared to duck quick if a hammer shaft came flying through the hoof reek if Jotty's birse was up, for he spent his busy life solving everybody's problems but his ain. Some blacksmiths had a reputation for their ill-nature and Jotty was no exception.

Jotty had just gotten the telephone and the linesmen had cut down the old chestnut tree where the wires came down from the pole to his parlour window. Jotty's wife was fair dumfoonert with the dirl of the thing in her lugs: farmers asking for Jotty or his man to come and look at their binder that wouldna bind a sheaf, or anither that wadna cut a stalk o' corn, and no wonder when you remembered that some of them stood outside all winter, rusting and rotting in the sleet and rain, with never a drop of oil or a clart of grease on the knotter mechanism or the cutting bar. What did they expect when they didn't look after their machinery!

Shoddy Davidson yonder biggit a ruck on top of his binder at the finish o' hairst, which at least kept it dry when he hadn't a shed to hold it in, and Jotty said a lot more of them could take a leaf out of Shoddy's beuk; lads like Spootiehowe and Snibbie Tam yonder, for you might still see last year's clyack sheaf sticking out of their binders in the middle of a stibble park, never even troubling themselves to take it to the gate, let alone transport it on the road – at least it was still there at the back of the New Year, the last time you was in that airt.

Snibbie Tam went over the parks to the Mains to ask for a bang on his telephone ('cause it was only the big farmers that had them) and he dialled Jotty's wife at breakfast time and said he liked the smell of her bacon frying that was coming over the line, just to humour her like, and said that a bicker of brose did fine with him, and when he heard a bit 'Ki-hee' of a laugh in his hairy lug he speired gin Jotty or his man would take a jump on his bike and come up to Kirniehole and take a gander at his binder, 'cause it wadna bind a sheaf, and when it did it was no thicker than a dog's leg, dammit tae hell.

But Jotty hadn't the time to go near Snibbie Tam, so the daft gowk yoked his three-horse binder in a yavel park and cut a whole day throwing loose sheaves. He was that anxious on sic a fine day (and there were few of them that year) and Jotty never putting in an appearance that the chiel went fair starkers. Hardly gave the horse beasts time for a munch of hay at dinner time, or a blibber of water, but had them trailed out of the stable and away to the hairst rigs as soon as he had a tattie over his ain thrapple, hardly taking time to chew it he was in such a fash. Next day he had everybody out gathering and binding up the sheaves, even the kitchie quine and his auld mither, and a tinker that was passing on the road. The tink happened to look over the dyke to see what the daft creatures were at, thinking maybe that Snibbie was scarce of binder-twine, or that he had been using an old back-delivery reaper. So Snibbie cried 'Hie' to the tink and the creature came over the stubble with his pack on his back and Snibbie said 'Can ye mak' a ban'?' And the tink said 'Aye, fine at,' and Snibbie said 'Weel, gie us a hand tae gether up this stuff.' So the tinker left his pack at the fairm hoose, where he got a bowl of hot soup from Snibbie's wife, and a fill to his pipe, and syne he got yoked to making bands and tying sheaves and stooking them, and right good he was at it too, and tidy in his work, and though it was a long sair trauchle of a hairst Snibbie kept him on for the leading, for he was a good hand with the fork as well, and he slept in the barn and got his food in the kitchen. Atween times,

15

when the weather was bad, Snibbie had the tink yoked to the Smiler, like a horse beast, with a rope over his shoulder, raking between the stooks, but when Snibbie was out of sight the tink turned the rake on its back, upside-down with its teeth in the air, so that he had an easier go and nearly ran off with the thing. Snibbie paid him three pounds a week for this, besides gathering strabs and opening out sheaves that were sprouting in the bands, so that as a hairst hand he made as much or more in three weeks than a loon got for a six months' fee.

So that was Snibbie, and he went right off his food that year of the bad hairst in 1927, the worst in living memory and there has never been the likes of it since, folk chauvin on till the New Year in the hairst parks and burning whole fields of corn when it was dry, not worth the cutting for all the corn that was left on the withered stalks. And Snibbie didn't sleep at nights for the batter of the rain at his windows and the thought of his corn sprouting in the stooks, and his wife was at her wits' end with the breet and right glad to see the end of that ill hairst and the stirks all chained up in the byres.

But never mind Snibbie though he be throu', for as far as Jotty was concerned the hairst was only startin', and a lot of binders still to be sorted.

But bad hairst or good, horses still died of grass sickness and beasts took ill and the vet was another lad that was sore tormented when the farmers got the telephone. There was old Johnny Rettie from the Myres that was seldom sober and cleverest when he was drunk. Johnny had the 'phone before the farmers, but now he regretted it, for they had him out of bed in his sark tail any hour of the night. But Johnnie's wife took over the 'phone, and as she had a sharpish tongue she soon sorted out the farmers and they thought twice about ringing her up at any hour of the day, and when this didn't work she stiffened the accounts a bit. She kept the books as well because Johnnie couldn't be bothered, and left to his own wyles the farmers would have had his services for nothing. In the old days of the shilt and gig Johnnie's sheltie knew all the places and took him there and back drunk or sober, but since he got a motor car he had to have a chauffeur to drive him about. And Johnnie would pull an aching tooth or lance a human boil or even deliver a bairn if he had to, and sometimes

16

save the doctor a lang journey to some ailing body who needed no more than a dose of salts and treacle.

But Johnnie was getting old and a bit dottled folk thocht and near the end of his tether, so they sometimes tried him out to see how clever he was or to see if he was losing any of his skill. Now there was a chiel they called the Wily Rottan who warsled on a place on the Hill o' Jock that had a mare with the colic, and when he 'phoned the vet Johnnie told him to put a sack on her nares, which meant over her back and rump to keep her warm or he came to see her. So the Wily Rottan told his foreman to put the sack on a healthy mare to play a prank on Johnny Rettie. Now the vet had a squeaky kind of voice, like he always had a greet in his throat, a fraiky kind of wye of speaking to animals, in a language they seemed to understand, and he had got into a habit of speaking to humans in the same tone, maybe because he thought them no better than animals sometimes, and whiles a bit worse. Anyway, when he got warsled out of his car and stytered over to the stable Wily's lads were waiting at the door to get a laugh at Johnnie, but he just smiled in the passing and went swaggering along the stable in his checked tweed suit looking at the mares, right to the far end of the stable, where five mares and a horse stood in a row. The sack was on the first mare in the third pair, fifth from the door, but Johnnie Rettie passed her by and came back to the second mare in the foreman's pair, went up beside her in the stall and took off his pickiesae hat and listened at her bellie with his best lug, poking at her ribs and flanks with his soft skilled fingers, syne he told the foreman to get hold of her head and put a stick in her mouth or he got a look at her teeth, for Johnnie was a dentist as well as a vet. 'That's the wrang ane,' says the Rottan, coming to the door and thinking to catch the vet off guard. 'But na na,' says Johnnie, like a bairn choked on his medicine, 'ye thocht ye wad play a trick on Johnnie Rettie, eh! But I'll tell ye this Wiley, that yer mearie's gaun tae hae a foalie!'

'I ken that,' says the Rottan, still crowing like a cock on the midden plank.

'Aye,' says the vet, with a bit sparkle in his cunning eye, 'but ye didna ken that she was gaun tae hae twa.'

'Twins vet?' Wiley asked, fair stamygastered.

'Aye twins Wiley; twa foalies, so I'll gie her a ballie and file doon her back teeth a bittie, so that she can chew better, and gin ye mend yer manners Wiley I'll maybe come back and foal the crater for ye.'

'God's sake vet, afore ye leave come owre tae the hoose for a dram.'

Now when Dargie Thomason saw the vet's car standing in the close at Wiley's place he sent his loon on his bicycle to tell the vet to come up to Sandyknowe 'cause he had a cow with the staggers.

'The staggers, loon,' said the vet.

'Aye,' says the loon, fair in earnest.

'And have ye been layin' on 'er wi' a stick, loon?'

'No, I hinna touched 'er!'

'Ah weel, tell yer father I'll be up juist noo,' said the vet, and went in with Wiley for his dram.

Up at Sandyknowe the vet met Dargie in the close and he took Johnnie to the byre to see the ailing cow.

'The wife canna melk 'er,' Dargie explained, 'she's aye tryin' tae mak' her watter and staggers aboot a' owre the place.'

Johnnie Rettie stood on the causey greep and glowered at the little black cow with mounting interest.'But gin she had the stag- gers Dargie she couldna stand ava, lat alane fit aboot. G'wa and get a basin o' warm watter and a bittie soap and we'll hae a look at her in-timmers.' And Johnnie Rettie took off his pickiesae hat and his jacket and gave them to his driver, then rolled up his sark sleeves and waited for Dargie with the hot water. When he re- turned the vet soaked his hands in the soapy water, and while Dargie held the cow's tail aside he thrust his bare arm full-length into the uterus of the ailing cow. After about five minutes he withdrew his hand and washed in the basin, then put on his coat and hat again.

'She'll nae trouble ye again Dargie,' he said, 'and she'll stand at peace to be milked.'

'What ailed her than, vet?' Dargie asked.

'Ye kent that yer cooie was in calf, Dargie?'

'Oh aye, I kent that vet.'

'Ah weel, the calfie had a wee foot in the water passage and she couldna mak' 'er watter properly, that's the wye she was staggerin' aboot. I've juist put the foot back in the womb and yer cooie will be a' richt noo Dargie.'

A skeelie mannie was Johnnie Rettie the folk said, and they knew they owed him a lot.

But all this time we've been with the vet Jotty the blacksmith has got the binders sorted and they're back in the hairst parks, transported from their bogey-wheels and ready for cutting. The canvasses have been buckled on to the elevator rollers, the blade sharpened and fixed to the driving-rod on the cutting-bar, the needle threaded and the driving wheel screwed doon, the divider in position and the platform adjusted.

The three-horse team are yoked to the drag-pole, the driver in his seat, the whip in a socket at his elbow, as long as a fishing-rod, though you never saw him using it. Maybe you could stand on the platform going round the first time, seeing there wasn't a job stooking, slicing round the stubble roads made by the scythemen, the corn reels striding into the standing grain, swathing it on to the cutting bar, the blade in lightning motion, slashing the feet from the ripened corn as it falls on the platform canvas, to be hustled into the guts of the machine, the packer arms grabbing furtively at the corn stalks, getting them into bundles with the ears to the tail of the binder, the wooden butter tidying the shear of the sheaf, the long steel needle curving up through to put a string round it from the canister under the driver's seat, the knotter tying it, the knife cutting the string, the delivery arms tossing the bound sheaves on to the shorn stubble at regular intervals, all as quick as the eye can follow, faster than human being could ever perform it. And as the long rows of sheaves increased so the stookers picked them up and set them on end, stubble to stubble, eight or ten sheaves to the stook, set north to south to catch the varying winds, the corn clustered to the sun and weather, row after row, park after park until the weather broke...

Then the noise and clatter of the binders ceased and you were yoked with scythes to cut the lying holes, corn that the rain had flattened and would choke the binders, so you bound the sheaves by hand and trailed them to the open stubble, where you stooked them clear of the standing crop. And the rain of 1927 was no ordinary rain for it fair lashed doon, not for days, but for weeks on end, almost non-stop, so that the grun wouldn't carry a binder, and some folks scythed whole parks and bound it by hand, the women sore trauchled at the binding. Others yoked their horse-mowers and cut it like hay, in long swaths that had to be gathered up and bound by hand; but it stood so long in the stook that the corn sprouted at the bands of the sheaves. Far away on the Buchan coast you could hear the growl and boom of the sea, like you had a buckie at your lug, and thousands of white gulls landed on your sheaves and stooks, filling their craps with your corn and vomiting the husk on your stubble, glued into little balls with their stomach spit, and your sheaves and stooks all whitened with their guano. 'Damned fishers' hens,' Hilly called them: 'I wish they'd bide at hame and ate their ain stinkin' herrin'!' But maybe Hilly forgot that the herring boats had all gone south to Yarmouth at this time o' the year and that the gulls had no other option but to turn on the farmers for a bite to eat. Yet it was the cushie-doos and the craws that Hilly and the Mains gunned doon and you'd never see them fire a cartridge at a herring gull, maybe because they minded the good things they did when the ploughing started, devouring all the grub and sic like beasties that damaged their crops in the spring-time.

So it was stook parade for the farming chiels, days and weeks of it, the most hated job in agriculture, re-setting stooks that had been set up many times before, blown down by the equinox winds or had simply collapsed from bad stooking; but whatever the cause a wearisome, disheartening, leg-weary ordeal, especially if you was sweating in oilskin suits, and the only consolation was to look over the hedge and see your neighbours at the same trauchle.

But as the sky loured and the days of rain lengthened you were driven inside to twine straw rapes between the empty stalls in the long double byre, or up in the corn loft if it were empty. The long cement greep gave you the full length of the byre to twine a rape without going outside to the wet, enough to wind a ball or cloo for the ruck thatchin' after hairst (if it was ever going to finish this year you wondered) and you twined and twined walking backwards all the time while the grieve or the foreman sat on a trochie at the far end of the byre and thrummed the straw through their fingers, further and further from your thraw-heuk, while the rape lashed the bare greep like a quine's skipping rope. The greep wasn't all that wide, so that if there were four of you on the job, with two rapes going at the same time you had to watch not to entangle them. The straw had been 'drawn' beforehand, plucked from the ribs of a ruck with your bare hands, a process that straightened the stalks and made better rapes for the thatching.

'Nae sae fast loon,' the grieve would cry when his rape had spun into a rottan's tail and snapped in the middle, so that he had to get up and splice it. So you kept your mind on the job for a while, away from the quines and moonlight trysts among the stooks. But there was a great art in letting out a straw rape, even and smooth through your fingers to form a trig and tidy rope, not a loose and hairy one that broke on the top of a ruck and made you nearly lose your balance. Making edrins was another ploy some lads excelled at, pear-shaped cloos that could be laced under the main rapes, forming a sort of net to keep the thatch in place in the howling winds of a winter's night.

When you had a great bing of cloos and edrins, enough you thought to rape the whole cornyard you could make a pair of ploo reins, using a thripple or three-pronged thraw-heuk and binder twine; thin ropes that were pliable in the horseman's hands, tight and hard till the oil oozed out of them in the twining, and a thicker pair of cart reins would come in handy, or great thick girdins that would rope a cart load of hay or straw, for you never bought ropes at a fairm toon.

And then the kitchie quine came in with the piece basket and a kettle of steaming tea, for at the Knock fairm you got a piece as long as the hairst lasted, fair or foul, though it were three months, including the ruck thackin' and the tattie liftin', be ye single or cottared, and maybe in return you'd do a bit of unpaid overtime when the weather cleared, an hour or two at the cutting or stooking in a fine evening, or an extra load of sheaves at the leading time, when the great big harvest moon would be rising cheerfully over the dew that was settling on the stubble fields. But there were some places where you didn't get a bite between diets unless you were actually harvesting, which made you hellish hungry when you weren't, and even for this you was expected to do a bit extra on a fine night, so the Knock was a good place to be at as far as this was concerned.

But sometimes if the price was promising Knockie would have the feeding byre half filled with thriving stots taken in from the grass parks to fatten on tares and green corn for the Christmas sales. So you would have to scythe the tares and cart them home to the turnip shed, about a cart load a day, mostly in the wet or dewy mornings or the stooks dried, while the horsemen would be oiling their binders or sharpening the blades and spreading the damp canvasses to dry on a stook, or maybe making ruck foons with the whin and broom you had cut around the quarry brae, or carting home the reeds and sprotts you had scythed and sheafed in the peat-bog. Oh aye, you never wanted for a job on a fairm-toon, fair or foul, and there was always the byre to lime-wash while it was empty, or sweep down the cobwebs from the rafters, and if the worst came you could always turn the sharn midden or wash the horse carts or clean out the dam. But if you had to twine rapes in the little bailie's byre they might be a bit shorter, because he sometimes had a shorter byre, with smaller stalls for young store cattle, and you was minded of the stranger who went to the fairm toon and the farmer chiel was showing him round the steading when out of a door and over the close goes a great strapping chiel, near twice the size of an ordinary body, and the stranger being impressed said: 'By Jove, but that's a fine figure of a man, and who might he be?' So the farmer listened to the iron heels of the lad on the causey stones and he says: 'Man, that's oor little bailie!' 'Good heavens,' says the stranger, polite like, him being of the gentry, 'if that's your small cattleman I should certainly like to see the big one!'

But the weather began to kittle up a bittie, blasts of wind that blew down your stooks again and a bit spunk of sun to dry the ground. But on clean land where grass had been sown in the wind couldn't move your stooks, because the grass had grown nearly up to the bands of your sheaves, and unless you threw them over on a fine day, to let the sun and wind get at the butts of the sheaves you were likely to get het rucks, for the damp grass would boil and steam in your stacks and ruin your grain samples. Then one fine dewy morning you'd see the rucks steaming and the fairmer chiel sticking his arm into the ribs of a ruck up to his elbow and pulling out a few stalks of corn or barley to feel if it was hot, and if it was on the lowe he'd be off to the telephone to the contractor lads to come and thresh it before it got worse. Or maybe he'd yoke his men to turning the rucks and making them smaller, sheaf by sheaf, to let them get the air, with a tripod in the middle to ease the pressure as the stack got bigger and heavier, which he should have done in the first place to prevent fermentation. Syne the chiel would go and blether to folk that he'd lost his gold watch in one of the rucks at the leadin', but he couldna mind which ane it was so the men were turning all the rucks you'd biggit to see if they could find it. But the story of the lost watch was getting a bit thin as an excuse for bad management and folk just took a bit snigger of a laugh behind your back and said it served you right for not shifting your stooks sooner and giving them a new stance on the grass before they got so sloppy.

And sometimes you'd see Hilly's lads throwing down a whole park of stooks on new grass stubble, old Hilly in his hat leading the foray, away out in front of his foreman billy, and him fair gnashing his teeth at Hilly for slaving him, every lad throwing down as many stooks as he could batter, rag-tag and bob-tail, mostly in the forenoon, just before the sun was at its highest, smiling down on Hilly's lads with their jackets off and sweating like tinks in a brawl. But you knew fine what Hilly was up to, for by the time the lads had gotten their dinner the sun and the wind would get at the butts of the sheaves and dry out the grass before Hilly stacked it in the afternoon.

And if Hilly thought he hadn't enough stooks flattened by dinner time for an afternoon's leading he'd yoke a cottar wife to ding doon the stooks, as he sometimes had a woman on the fork anyway, pitching up the sheaves to the carts. But woe betide if tho rain came on again about piece time and Hilly had knocked down too many stooks, for the men would have to put on their oilskin suits and set them all up again, and yon foreman chiel would be cursing like hell and speiring where was thon lad with the hat that was in sic a hurry tearing down the stooks, for you'd never see Hilly setting them up again, and most likely he'd have a cooie to calve or a sooie to pig, or some such lame excuse to keep him out of sight or things simmered down a bittie. But the lads at the stookie knew fine that Hilly would be in the kitchen, with his hat on a peg and his feet on the mantelshelf, reading the daily paper – Buchan Leer or the Ellon Squeak, and not even a cat kittlin', let alone a coo.

But there was no meal and ale for 1927, or very few, and some single billies finished the rakings at one place and left at the November Term, only to find at their next place that the hairst was still unfinished.

There are no Meal and Ales nowadays, when you got your bowl of sowens that you supped with a horn-spoon, with maybe a sixpence in the bottom of the empty bowl if you were lucky. The real Meal and Ales disappeared with the horse wark, and when the tractors started folk called them Harvest Home Festivities; a sort of dinner and dance among the bigger farmers, known as the annual Farmers' Ball. The Kirk has upheld tradition with its yearly Harvest Thanksgiving, when the walls are decorated with corn dollies and the congregation brings gifts for the poor, like sacks of potatoes, flowers and vegetables, and the poor nowadays are known as the Old Age Pensioners. The whole thing is a bit of a sham anyway, for it is sometimes held when there are still acres of bales on the stubble fields, and parks of wasted corn and barley yet to be harvested. 1927 was a bit like that; when you didn't know where to draw the line, some folk finished and some folk not, and some others so disgusted they never bothered with Meal and Ale.

But whatever Meal and Ales were going that year old Jotty the blacksmith would be there, his fiddle under his chin, scraping away with the bow, a dram at his elbow, and nothing further from his mind than binders.

'Dammit tae hell,' he would hiccough, 'a body maun hae some fun!'

And the farmer billies of the Bogside would put their heads together and hire a contractor and thresh his three stacks of grain, for they knew they would be clean lost without Jotty the blacksmith, though he signed himself in their accounts as Jonathan McGillivray.

Johnnie Rettie got an invitation to the Meal and Ale on the Wylie Rottan's place on the Hill o' Jock; maybe because he had promised the Rottan twa foalies when he was only lookin' for one. After the feastin' on roast turkey and the suppin' of sowens and a good dram Wylie asked the vet to say a few words by way of a speech, most likely because he knew that Johnnie Rettie would say something to make them all laugh and raise the spirits of the company.

So the vet dabbed his moustache with his white hankie, for there was no such thing as a table napkin at Wylie's place, and then rose up from his chair, a bit unsteadily at first, until he got stanced, while his wife held on to the tail of his jacket, ready to give it a sharp tug if he said anything out of place, which wasn't uncommon with Johnnie Rettie when he had a good dram in.

He began with a few serious words on the ill hairst they had just experienced, the worst that he could mind on he said since he came to the Bogside, near forty years back, and it was the first time he had ever seen snow on the stooks, or the ploughing so late in starting, and he hoped for the sake of everybody concerned that he would never live to see it again, whereupon some of the billies cried 'Hear, hear!' and Johnnie glowered at them from under his glasses and took another sip of his whisky.

But not all harvests were bad, the vet continued, sticking his thumbs in the waistcoat pockets of his natty grey suit; not all harvests were bad, and he could mind on the farmer cheil who had such a grand hairst that he held a ball at the end of it, not just a Meal and Ale like Wylie here, but a grand affair in the barn and folk were invited from miles around to come and have a fling. Now this farmer cheil had an affa ugly dother near thirty years old who had never been kissed or cuddled in her life, nor even winked at by the working cheils on her father's farm. So the farmer told his quine to dress up well for the occasion and maybe she would get a lad in the leith of it.

A lot of folk turned out for the ball, farmers and their wives and their sons and daughters, besides some of the working cheils and kitchendeems for miles aroon, and some of them came without invitation, just for the fun of the thing and all were made welcome.

But not a lad speired for the farmer's daughter, nor asked her up for a dance, so the quine was a bit crestfallen in all her finery, and when all the folk had gone she broke down and wept. 'But never mind quine,' her father said, offering her his hankie to dry her tears, 'next year we'll hold another ball for ye, and maybe ye'll have better luck next time.'

The next hairst wasn't all that to blow about, but the farmer cheil held a ball just the same and a hantle of folk attended it. The lassie dressed herself brawly and practised her steps for the dance but she fared no better than the year before. She sat the whole evening on the weighing machine in her fine clothes and watched the others enjoying themselves, while never a lad gave her a second glance in the passing nor asked her for a dance. The farmer cried out several times for a Ladies' Choice, and though the quine got a birl or two from the lads she picked up they just ignored her afterwards and went back to their more amorous partners.

It was a disappointing experience for farmer and daughter but as the next year's harvest came on the quine thought she would have another go, another last try to get a lad, even though it was only a farm servant – maybe she would be third time lucky. But as the winter drew on and her father never making a move she asked him if he was going to have another ball for her.

'Na na,' says he, fed up to the teeth looking for a lad for his ill-faured dother: 'Na na, if ye canna get a man wi' twa balls ye're nae likely tae get ane wi' three!'

Johnnie Rettie's wife gave his jacket a tremendous tug that pulled him down in his chair. Her face was as long as a decanter, with never a smile to pattern it. She knew most of his stories but this was a new one she had never heard before; harmless enough when he started but the ending caught her by surprise. But whatever his wife thought the folk fair skirled with laughter, especially the women, and thanks to their vet it hadn't been such a bad harvest after all, for all its trauchle.

Man in a Loud Checked Suit

Now Forbie Tait of Kingask never knew it but although he had fee-ed you to work for him body and soul (shades of *Uncle Tom's Cabin*) in that he had every ounce of your physical effort and some of your mental activity – taking a fervent interest in his cattle beasts and in pulling his turnips (or so he probably imagined) but actually, and mentally at least, Forbie had only engaged part of your energies, because most of the time only part of your mind worked for Forbie and the best of your thoughts were far away on higher things. Had this not been so, or in other words – if you had conformed to the frigidity of rustic life, contenting yourself with its dullness and monotony, harnessing your mind to its soulless illiteracy, its almost sterile simplicity – then people like Forbie Tate and Badgie Summers would never have existed beyond their mortal deaths, whereas your enlightenment has enabled you to breathe new life into their dry bones, to give them flesh and muscle and blood in the brain cells of readers yet unborn; to bring them alive that were dead, and surely this is the greatest glory that man can achieve, in the image of God, his maker, in resurrection.

When you was spreading muck or pulling turnips on the brae above the farm you was there only half the time, and only part of you at that, and not the better part, for your heart and soul was with the arts in whatever form you could find them: whether in books or magazines or even newspapers; films, posters or gramophone records, and as radio was just beginning to catch on in the cottar houses it didn't have much of your attention. You might be flinging muck about you with nothing further from your mind than sharn, your thoughts away with Jack Hulbert and Renate Muller in that wonderful British musical of the early 'thirties *Sunshine Susie*, with its delightful songs and dances, its carefree youthfulness and its music bringing an exuberant glow into your drab life; putting a lilt in your voice as you sang to yourself on the brae, the shit flying about you, your thoughts enlarging on the subject the more you dwelt on it, for days at a time, like being in love with someone beautiful beyond dreams, until the vision faded and lost its colour and left you with a pleasant memory, which is the accolade and surely the ultimate of which the human soul is capable. On the wings of song you might call it, when your thoughts are extrovert, going out to meet the world on the wings of angels; but woe betide when your thoughts become introvert, turning in upon yourself in a deep depression, when your angels come home to roost, drooping their feathers, in the simple Freudian thesis of melancholia. Being eccentric is like being on a tightrope, performing to an applauding audience, a delightful experience so long as you don't fall off, with only a frail net to catch you.

When Forbie Tait thought you was being punctual in the byres you was mentally in the projection box of some imaginary cinema screening the *Pathe Gazette* or the *Movietone News* on the stroke of eight; indeed your regularity at work was inspired by the consistency of the newsreel people in keeping up to date with world affairs. The bread and butter efforts of the film producers made everything worth while, and if the Hollywood moguls produced a masterpiece you was elated. Without the cinema backdrop in your daily drudgery you was without a guiding star, and if ever there was a round peg in a square hole you was the kingpin. But of course Forbie Tait knew nothing of the workings of your mind but he said he liked a lad who was punctual in the byres feeding his nowt. He even mentioned it to Badgie the foreman that you was punctual and conscientious and that he was pleased enough with your work. So long as you did your work Forbie didn't much concern himself with your own private pursuits. But it was the movies that turned you on so to speak, and made you tick, and you couldn't have cared less for the running of Kingask. That you had given a good performance was automatic; a means to an end, without enthusiasm for the daily drag.

During your second harvest on the place Badgie Summers taught you how to build a corn stack. Maybe he was just tired of crawling on the corn rucks and wanted a change. Anyway he took the cart you was driving and put you on the stack and showed you where to lay your sheaves, round by round from the inner circle, with plenty of hearting in the middle and a gentle slope to the outer edge, Badgie forking all the time and directing you right to the topmost pinnacle of the stack, then gave you a hand to rope and secure it against wind and weather, and you came down the ladder gratified, proud of your achievement.

It was quite a feat Badgie had taught you, the beginning of your stack-building career that was to last for thirty odd years, in which time you was to build an average of forty or fifty a year, depending on the size of the various farms you worked on, or the sum total of something like two-thousand corn, wheat and barley stacks, besides an experiment in flax building during the war, until the combines came in during the 'sixties and killed this skilful art. It was one job that gave you a pride in your work over many difficult years; a prestige and reputation with the farmers and sometimes though not often an extra pound or two to your meagre wages, besides a better chance of finding a job.

That was something you had to thank Badgie Summers for, him that was foreman at Kingask; otherwise you can't think how you would have managed it, or even made a start, and because of the art involved (or architecture if you like) it turned out to be a job you became really fond of, in spite of your aversion to farming in general. But when Forbie saw the stack you had built he told Badgie he'd better thrash it first in the season in case it watered. Badgie said there was no fear of that but knowing the old man he had to comply with his wishes.

Kingask kept a lot of hens; thousands of them, in sheds of weather-boarding scattered over the grass parks. Forbie believed in a policy of mixed farming, so that if one project failed the other might support it: just as some beef-cattle farmers went in for sheep or pigs as a sideline so old Forbie went in for hens. Young Tom was chief poultryman, with a fee-ed loon from the village to help him out, the two of them with a pony and cart filling the feed hoppers and the water fountains, mucking out the sheds and collecting the eggs. Tom's two sisters, Deborah and Edith, cleaned and packed the eggs into crates for the shops, and a van called twice a week to collect them. Badgie was on regular call to move a henhouse from one park to another, sometimes in the snow, or to take it home for repairs, for Tom was something of a joiner as well as many other things and good with his hands and a kit of tools. And Badgie would hitch the yokes and swingletrees to the hooks on the shed runners, like a sledge, and Jug and Kate would haul it out at the gate and over the road to where Tom wanted it in another park, mostly not far from the steading, so that he could take a rifle shot at the crows and the cushie-doos that hovered round the feed troughs. Tom and the loon had a steady job cleaning out these hen-arks, and the only time you was involved was on wet days, when Forbie whistled you home from the parks, and you went up to the corn loft, mixing feed, with a heap on the floor all the colours of the rainbow as you emptied it from the sacks; then turned it over and over until the colours dissolved into a whole of slatey grey, when you shovelled it back into the sacks again for feeding in the parks.

Though there was no electricity on the farms Tom was experimenting with the new incubators to raise their own chickens, maintaining the heat with oil lamps, as he did with the brooders after hatching, thus making a lot of the broody hens redundant and easing the work load in replacing the stock. Good laying breeds were selected and crossed with suitable cockerels. Tom also had a go at the battery-hen system, with the birds all in cages, food and water in front of them and laying their eggs where they stood; imprisoned for life and never out in the fields for a healthy scratch with other birds, and mostly their life-span ended with their moulting, when they were culled from their cages and taken to the butcher's shop, which was a good thing when it happened at Christmas time, because the cottars got a hen for dinner in the leith of it. Old Forbie didn't like this new-fangled idea of caging the birds for life and thought it was proper cruelty. He complained also of the lack of colouring in the egg yolks and thought there was something lacking in their diet. 'By gum,' he said, rocking his false teeth, 'it's nae natural keepin' hens in there Tom; and besides, foo wad ye like tae be keepit in they cages a' yer born days and never seein' a member o' the opposite sex?' But being a bachelor himself Tom had a ready answer for his old man. 'What ye never had ye never miss,' he said, glimmering through his glasses, with a wink to the loon who was standing beside him.

But even without the hen Christmas and New Year were grand times at Kingask. The cottars got a cherry cake from Mrs Tait, and a big fancy tin packed with cream biscuits, with sweeties for all the bairns. Even the tin was a luxury and Kathleen kept it for years to hold her oatcakes, because she liked the crinolined lady on the lid, and the sights of London round the sides, Buckingham Palace and all that. Even in those so-called Hungry 'Thirties it is a fact that fruit cake was so cheap from the grocers' vans you were still eating it half through January; every time you had tea you had currant or sultana cake, till you was scunnered at the sight of it and glad to get back to loaf and treacle, oatcakes and stovies, peasemeal brose and porridge. Bread and fancy cakes of all kinds were also cheap and plentiful, in fact the pound sterling was so elastic it could be stretched to such an extent that when people were sensible there was no real hardship in the cottar household, except perhaps in the bigger families, though these were tending to get smaller. Whisky and beer were unheard of except in the pubs (which you never visited) but wine and soft drinks were easily got, provided you returned the bottles. Tobacco and cigarettes were at throwaway prices and smoking was fashionable. Very few women smoked or drank and most of the men smoked pipes filled with thick black twist.

Your first Christmas at Kingask was the best one, maybe because there was snow on the ground and all the countryside like one big Christmas card standing wide open; even without the trees, for there were no trees in the wind-torn parish of Pittentumb, except for a few survivors at the manse of Peatriggs and the old ruined castle of Spitullie. But the blue of the sea and the white of the land was a dream in bone china, the sky feathered with wind-blown cloud and ramparts of snow on the far horizon. The sea itself was surly, grumbling all day against the land, with a deeper tone in the boom of the surf; angry at night when the tide rose in a snarl of sleet, stabbed by the lighthouse beam from Brochan, swinging over the sea and the parks. It swept the braes at Kingask on the darkest nights, without a star in the sky, showing you up like a thief in a searchlight, lurching home with an old fencing post to light your fire, so everybody was honest at Kingask, or what you took was in daylight (which wasn't very much) but then nobody suspected you.

It was cold on the feet while you plucked turnips on the brae, jerking them out of the steel hard earth with a twin-pronged adze (for want of a better description) your mittened hands stinging with frost, though the sun shone warmly at noon, slanting across the snow in an autumn glow, crystallizing the crusted fields like champagne in amber glasses. Folks were driving out fresh dung on the snow, warm and steaming from the sharn middens, the smell of it like perfume on the brittle air. The hairs of your nostrils froze like spikes and your breath rose like steam in front of your face; your ears anaesthetized, while your shadow dodged behind you like a man on the run. There was nothing for it but action to keep the blood going, work or starve, and as there was only one day off at Hogmanay there was no excuse for feeling the cold. With plenty of food in your belly you never really felt the cold, which was easy at New Year time with all the titbits, but at other times with the long drag between meals your stomach ached for food, for there were no tea breaks. Even though you had your own house you daren't be seen with a snack and a thermos flask; such a liberty had not yet come into fashion, though it did later. Meantime you would sometimes sneak in by your cottage and gulp down a cup of tea and a bun Kathleen had ready for you when you left the turnip field, going home to the byre. You just hoped that Forbie or the women folk hadn't seen you from the farmhouse windows when you left the cottage, for though it was only five minutes of truancy it was frowned upon and you didn't want to be caught in the act. The farmhouse of Kingask stood like a sentinel over the parks and you was never out of sight of its peering windows. Whether they saw you or not nothing was said, but you didn't push your luck too far just in case, and sometimes you missed your fly-cup if you saw anyone in the farm close, or if Forbie whistled you home earlier for a shower of rain.

But in spite of the cold and hunger, hard work and frustration, you had one other consolation – you was a film fan and Garbo and Harlow were at their loveliest, filling your skies with their radiance, larger than life itself in those days of your youth, though now in your old age you can see you was only chasing shadows, for the cine film is only shadows reflected on a bed-sheet. But in those days they were real enough and the Empire

Theatre in London was offering three-thousand seats daily at one-and-sixpence each to watch them: Garbo as *Camille* (Lady of the Camellias) and Harlow in *Red Dust* – and you had never heard of such riches from such beauty and wished you'd been a film producer, far from the neep parks, the snow and the sharn. Film going was becoming a religion in the realms of angels, and the women had gods in the shape of Clark Gable, Robert Taylor and Spencer Tracy. Shirley Temple was everybody's child and now they were adopting Little Lord Fauntleroy; Deanna Durbin sang at the gates of Paradise while Bing Crosby was catching *Pennies from Heaven*. Frank Capra had found his *Lost Horizon* and Cecil B. de Mille had made *The Sign of the Cross*. Claudette Colbert had bathed in asses milk and we had seen *The Last Days of Pompeii*. Sonja Henie had just cut the figure 8 on silver skates and Paul Muni was digging in *The Good Earth*. But the crowning glory was the coronation of King George VI and Queen Elizabeth in colour, shown all over the country on the day it took place, May 12th 1937, almost as quick as television, and old Forbie was obliged to give you the day off to watch it in Brochan, seeing it was a national holiday. There had been three Kings on the British throne within a year: George V, Edward VIII and George VI, whereupon Forbie remarked: 'By gum, ye get a new keeng ony day o' the week nooadays!'

It was during your second summer at Kingask that old Forbie ran short of hens corn, having sold too much for seed in the spring. This wouldn't have mattered to you at all but for the fact that you couldn't get corn for your own hens. Badgie Summers had been wiser than you or better informed and had bought a bag in advance, before the shortage became acute. He didn't have to worry about hen feed but he told you where you could buy a bushelful to tide you over till harvest time, up at Stovie Roger's place, beyond the smiddy; so off you set one sunny evening with an empty sack on your bicycle and five bob in your pocket to visit Stovie Roger. What Badgie didn't tell you was that Stovie would speir you inside out before he would give you the corn: your name and where you came from and why you couldn't get corn from the farmer you worked for? – and why come to him for corn when there were so many other places where you could have got it? He also wanted to know where you had worked

33

be-fore you came to Kingask? – How long you had been there and why you had left it? He even wanted to know where your parents lived and your wife's folk; where they lived and what they all did for a living? You told him they were all cottar folk, but you felt like telling him he could keep his bludy corn and maybe you would get it from somebody with better manners and who was less inquisitive; though you could by no means be sure of this in a scarcity round about Kingask, where you was still a comparative stranger and everybody had to know about your dirty washing and the size of your shoes and whether or not you slept with your wife before they would trust you out of their sight, or part with the dirt under their nails on your behalf. Badgie Summers had qualified for such trust and respect after twelve years as foreman at Kingask, while you was only banging the door knocker.

But at last, after about an hour of interrogation, Stovie was satisfied that you wasn't a born thief: that you wasn't just spying out the place and where the dog slept, and that you wouldn't come sneaking back some dark night and steal his hens or a sackful of peats or set fire to his stack-yard or let the water out of his dam – or even sleep with his kitchiedeem – for such a thing was not unheard of, even among married men. Stovie also seemed to be convinced that you hadn't just escaped from the convict prison or the lunatic asylum and that you was really fee-ed at Kingask, though it was a wonder he didn't ask the colour of old Forbie's eyes, just to make sure; or what was his swear word, and you felt sure that if he'd had a telephone, and Kingask had one, he would have rung up Forbie to ask for your credentials.

So you went up to the loft with Stovie and he filled you a bushel of corn, strake full, that means he took a broken fork shaft (though some folk used a scythe – broad or scythe-straik – hence the 'strake') and scraped it over the rim of the wooden bushel, scraping off the surplus corn, to make sure you didn't get a grain of it more than you was entitled to, but just for bonus he licked his thumb and picked up two ears of corn from the loft floor, sticking to his moistened thumb print, and flicked them into the bushel, then tipped the lot into the empty sack you held out for him. He took the two half-crowns you offered him and put them in his waistcoat pocket, while you clambered down the loft stair and set the half sack of corn across your handlebars, then jumped on your bike, Stovie watching you with the dog beside him till you was clear of his premises and on to the main road, bound for Kingask.

Next day you told Badgie your experience and he said that was what you would expect from Stovie Roger, but that he was one of the best farming chiels in the parish of Pittentumb, and that he never missed a Sunday at the kirk; which gave you a mighty poor opinion of the farmers round about Kingask, and even less regard for the folk that filled the kirk at Peatriggs. But when you told Badgie this he said: 'Tyoo fie man; it was Stovie that put the clock in the spire o' the kirk, paid for it himsel', so that folk would mind on him, and of course he's an elder!'

The story went around about Stovie, that before the Rev. Thow came to Peatriggs he complained to the former minister about a kitchiedeem from one of the farms who came to the kirk on Sundays with a plunging neckline. So the minister had a word with the quine in the vestry after service and explained to her that one of the elders had lodged a complaint about her low-necked dress and wondered perhaps if she could possibly wear something less revealing. Personally he had to admit to himself that she certainly had something to display and he had no objection. Trust Stovie Roger to go and spoil things, because from where the lassie sat in the congregation the minister had an unclouded view of the valley of sunshine and could have tossed a pandrop nearly down to her navel. But the lassie insisted that she wore a low neckline because her lad liked to see her dressed like that and she wasn't going to change it to please a narrow-minded kirk elder, whoever he may be, or though it had been the Laird o' Pittentumb himsel'. She said that when she lay down in that dress and her lad put his head on her bare breast and listened he said he could hear the angels singin'. But the minister wasn't convinced of this and said he would have to try it himself before he would believe it. So the lass lay down on the vestry couch and the minister knelt beside her and laid his lug on her naked bosom. After a while he looked up and said: 'I canna hear ony angels singin', lassie – but maybe I'm on the wrang wavelength?'

'Och no Reverend,' said the quine, now flushing to the lips:

'It's nae that; ye couldna hear them that wye – ye're nae plugged in!'

This was the minister who got on a bus from Brochan and unavoidably sat down beside a drunk. After a while the drunk became abusive and the minister upbraided him and said he should think shame of himself going home to his wife and bairns in a state like that. But the drunk argued that he wasn't all that bad and at least he didn't have his collar on back to front like the minister. 'But look at me as an example,' said the man in black, 'I am never drunk!'

'Never drunk,' said the man; 'nae even on Communion Sundays on a' that wine that's left efter the service?'

'Least of all on Communion Sabbath,' said the minister, 'for on that day I am the father of thousands!'

'The father of thoosands! Gweedsake Reverend, it's yer breeks ye shid hae on back tae front, nae juist yer collar!'

Now you was a member of the Peatriggs kirk yourself by now, having changed your membership from your last place when you came into the parish, though you hadn't gone very often, only twice the year before to the communions. But now Kathleen wanted little Brian baptized. She wanted it done before she had another one, because she was with child again, and it would be born sometime in the spring. But you would have to get a new suit. You couldn't go to the kirk in your marriage suit nowadays; you had worn it so often to go everywhere on your bicycle that the arse of your breeks was polished smooth as a bus driver's seat, the lapels of the jacket sticking out like a donkey's ears, the pocket lids dog-eared, the trouser legs creased like a melodeon, the knees paper thin; in fact Stovie Roger had a better suit on his scarecrow, but since he took it inside every night there was little chance of stealing it. So you would have to get a new suit, which meant you would have to ask a half-day off from Forbie (which was like asking for the Pole-star) because the tailors in the toon closed their shops about the same time as you shut your byre doors at Kingask, so you'd have to go and get measured on a Saturday afternoon.

But Forbie was in a thraw that summer about half-days off and rather than let you go he'd have you sheiling the sods from the verge of the farm road, or cresoting henhouses with a tar brush, seeing he was short of work, rather than see you off on your bike or away with the wife and the pram to the toon, no matter what your errand was. Maybe he thought you'd just be spending your money anyway and better to keep you at home where you might be saving it, the little you had. It was Badgie's week-end with the cows that you asked off to buy your suit, thinking that this would be most convenient, and you had expected that Badgie would be about the place on the Saturday afternoon. But as things would have it Badgie and his wife had a wedding that day and couldn't oblige you. You could have waited another fortnight but you was anxious to have the suit before the christening. You told Forbie all this but even though he was an elder of the kirk himself he wouldn't let you off. It was like trying to brasso the moon while it was still full, before the waning started, wondering how you would get up there in the first place. Forbie made the excuse that Badgie being off as well there wouldn't be an able-bodied man about the place for a whole afternoon; and what if the beasts 'ran a heat' (tormented with gadflies) and broke out of the parks, or the place caught fire – what was he going to do? There was some sense in what Forbie said and you could see his point of view; but you said you would be gone for only a couple of hours or so and you would be back by cow time at the latest. All the same it wasn't the done thing Forbie said and he wouldn't budge. Now it was said of Forbie Tait that he prepared for the day he would never see, and that he feared the death he would never die, and you was beginning to see the truth of it. And besides there were enough of them left about the place to run for help or cope with these unlikely disasters: what with young Tom and his sisters, the hen loon, the kitchie quine and the mistress, and old Forbie himself – enough of them to herd a whole park of nowt or pish out a fire before it got started. So you just ignored Forbie on the Saturday and never turned up in the stable for orders after dinner, but dressed yourself and went sailing down the brae on your bike for the toon.

Now you hadn't had a decent suit for a long time and you was determined to have a good one while you was about it; not a really expensive one but the best you could afford. But the tailors in Brochan had nothing on the hooks to fit you: neither Hepworths nor Claude Alexander nor Burtons; not enough padding to bolster your sloping shoulders, too wide in the waist or too narrow across the chest; too short in the arms or too long in the legs, and anything that sort of fitted you wasn't the right colour. Nothing for it but have one made to measurement, and you settled with Claude Alexander to have it done, seeing he was 'Scotland's National Tailor', and they measured you up and gave you a book of patterns from which to choose your colour, something you was about as good at as picking out the separate colours of the rainbow, and you should have had Kathleen there to help you. Now you'd had nothing but dark brown and deep blue suits ever since you'd come out of short breeks: 'cottar broon or fisher blue', as they were called, something you could always put on for a wedding or a funeral, seeing it was the only decent suit you could afford, and your old one would be good enough for 'Go-ashore' purposes as they said, like feeing markets or roups or Saturday nights at the pubs, or in your case for going to the pictures. But you was tired of all the Dismal Johnnies and thought that for once you'd have something brighter; something that would set the fashion in Pittentumb, and to hell with convention and poverty.

So you choose a loud check for your suit that would dispel all this gloom of mortal living and set a new image for the farm workers: away from the Hodden Grey and Kersey Tweed, Blue Serge and moleskin that had dominated the attire of the Scottish farm worker from the days of Burns and James Hogg, and you supposed that English farm workers were much the same. But you later discovered you had chosen something that no self respecting horseman or stockman, married or single, drunk or sober, would have the effrontery to be seen in, either at fair or market, kirk or ploughing match. What you had chosen was something for the Chep-Johns at Aikey Fair they said, or the swanks down in London yonder; or what the Laird or the factor might wear on the twelfth of August for the grouse shooting, but certainly not on a Sunday for the kirk at Peatriggs. Maybe you had gone too far because you had never thought of this when you chose the colour of your suit; so eager was you to be unortho-dox it was nearly a week before it struck you that you would be an oddity in a suit like that to be seen anywhere, never mind the

38

kirk. You was about thirty years ahead of your time with the suit but you would have to stick to your guns now and nail your colours to the mast. It was too late to mend matters because the tailors would be busy on the cloth by now with their long shears. Nor could you afford to buy another suit length and you had already deposited £2 on the one you'd chosen. Kathleen laughed outright when you told her of your discomfiture. She said you could dye it but that seemed silly, and she added that you should have had more sense. Who did you think you was anyway? – Clark Gable or the Laird of Cock-pen? Maybe you should have bought a kilt when you was about it. So you got little sympathy from Kathleen.

The tailors had promised to have the suit ready in a fortnight, and that you could pay by instalments if you wanted to. It cost you £8 ten shillings but Kathleen said she could afford to pay it cash from money saved from your monthly wage of £4. Forbie hadn't said anything about not turning up for work that Saturday, and as you had returned about four o'clock in the afternoon and had changed into your working clothes and was driving in your cows at the usual time for milking he let it slip. When you told him you wanted another couple of hours off to collect the suit a fortnight later he was less thrawn and said you could go. On the Sunday morning after breakfast you was in high spirits about your suit and wanted to try it on. Kathleen said it was just grand: a smashing suit with a waistcoat, and she had a shirt and tie to go with it, and she said you never looked better in your life, and she put her arms round your neck and kissed you, which made you feel like a million dollars, in movie language. She had just bought you a new armchair, because the stuffing was sticking out of your old one, and she had paid for it in Brochan from a surrendered insurance policy you couldn't afford. Seated in your new armchair with the Picturegoer was like the first sweet smell of success; if only you had been a film producer instead of a clod-hopper, and Kathleen had been your leading lady. Of course you never told Kathleen about your ambition to be a film director; nor did you discuss any of your thoughts with her about the movies, though she was bound to think it strange that you had all these film magazines lying about, and did a bit of writing on the sly, reading Shakespeare and all that sort of thing, which most other lads forgot about as soon as they left school. Not at all like her brothers you was and most likely a bit 'picter daft' as folk said, though she stuck up for you if anyone tried to make fun of it in her hearing. But your suit was fine she said and first class material, if only you had chosen a less gaudy colour. What would all the kirk folk think when they saw you in a braw thing like that? But this annoyed you, and you said to hell with the kirk folk and got up from the chair and put on the checked cap you had bought to go with the suit and strode out of the house, up the road for a stroll. And who should you meet but Forbie, on his Sunday morning round of the parks, and when he saw you in the brash new suit he nearly fell over the dyke he was straddling, but saved himself with his staff. 'By gum,' he said, nearly dropping his pipe from his mouth, 'but that's a braw mornin'!' If he had said: 'That's a braw suit!' you might have felt heartened, but as it was you had scarcely noticed what sort of morning it was, until Forbie drew your attention to it, when you was aware of the sun blazing down and that the dirt flies were everywhere and the sea blue and calm and motionless, with scarcely a murmur from its tumble on the beach. But you knew by the way that Forbie went hytering down the road that he couldn't get home fast enough to tell the women folk about the daft like suit the bailie lad had bocht.

You was that abashed that you put off your visit to the kirk as long as you could, leaving it till the sacrament Sunday, when you had no other option or excuse, especially when you wanted the Rev. Thow to baptize little Brian later on, so you would have to face the music. As it was you had left it a bit late because he had started swearing and you was worried about what he might say when the minister poured the cold water on to his head. You couldn't say where he had learned the swear words because you seldom swore yourself, something you was real particular about, and so was Kathleen, but as soon as the bairn could speak 'Bugger' and 'Damn' were among the first words he used; and even worse from time to time, and when you tried to check him he swore the worse, until you had him in tears. Nor could you any longer discuss something private in his hearing, or speak about the folk next door, or he up and told them about it and you didn't know where to look to avoid their reaction, your faces

40

crimson with guilt. Spelling out the words puzzled him however and you got away with that.

On the Sunday morning of the Sacrament, when the pair of you were rigged for the kirk, Kathleen took the poker and rapped on the back of the grate with the point of it, to let the Summers folk know you was ready, when young Esma came round for the bairn, fair delighted like a quine would be, and the four of you walked up the road for the kirk, Kathleen in her blue and white hairy coat, like the hide of a New-Foundland dog, and a trim little hat like a brose caup with a rim on it, and Mrs Summers rigged out as black as the Ace of Spades, with an enormous hat spiked with feathers and draped with sequins, both with bibles in their black gloved hands, while you and Badgie walked behind, pipes in mouth past the smiddy, where the blacksmith was rigging a granny on his lum, and he cried to Badgie to put in a good word for him at the kirk, seeing he would be needing it, working on the Lord's day. Within sight of the kirk you put your pipes away, and although you was a bit self-conscious in your new suit you was now determined to go through with it bold as brass. You was a bit early and stood about the door a minute, newsing to the farm folk, getting out of their cars and gigs and some on foot. A lot of them you had never seen before, or if you had you had forgotten them, and one of them in particular came over and shook hands with you, nice as ninepence and asking how you liked to farm Pitburn, thinking you was the new tenant of the place, until Stovie Roger comes over and tells him you was cottared at Kingask, when the man dropped your hand like it was a blighted potato and turned his back as quickly and spoke to somebody else, being taken aback with your new suit.

The bell began to ring and Stovie took his gold watch out of his waistcoat pocket and checked it with the clock he had biggit into the kirk tower and said we should be moving inside, reminding you to hand in your sacrament token in the porch beside the collection plate, Stovie being the elder for your corner of the parish. The inside of the kirk was like a cathedral (though you had never seen the inside of a cathedral) with bare stone walls and candlesticks on the altar and brass lamps hanging on long chains from the roof. While the kirk was filling up some folk sat with bowed heads while others glowered at everybody coming up the aisles, so you had time to look around at all the plaques on the walls in memory of the former ministers of the parish, and some of the bigger farmers, now deceased, though none of the Laird's folk were to be seen in this corner of Pittentumb, and maybe they had a private chapel and burial ground at Bogenchero. Outside you could still hear the bell ringing, high on the belfry, crying out to the heathens of the parish to 'Come awa', Come awa',' until the bellman changed his hand on the rope, when it said, very distinctly 'Ye're ahin, ye're ahin;' 'Collection, Collection!' until he got the swing of the rope and the rhythm again. Now you could feel the throb of the organ, playing ever so sweetly, like you sometimes heard it in some of the bigger cinemas, until the Rev. Thow appeared in his surplice, ready to partake of the Lord's Supper. He took his sermon from the fifty-third chapter of Isaiah, in a language that the patient folk of Pittentumb could understand, and in the declamation of it you would have heard the proverbial dropping of a pin, or better still, the gritting of a ewe's teeth chewing the cud. The Rev. Thow was an excellent reader of scripture, you could see that from the start, lifting his text from the Old Testament in a voice so clear and distinct that every word was like a falling dew drop; like the clisp of shears in snow white wool, the rasp of scythe in ripened corn, the clop of hoof on causey stones, the fall of a chain on byre cement, or the chop of axe on wood-block; and then he called them to repentance: 'For though your sins be as scarlet,' he cried, 'yet they shall be as white as wool,' and the folk of Pittentumb remembered the shearing, and could identify themselves with what the Rev. Thow was driving at. He led them in the green pastures by the quiet waters and in the shadow of death he gave a comforting hand; filled their cups to overflowing with the wine of everlasting life.

'Who hath heard our report?' the Rev. Thow was asking, gazing out over his congregation, pausing in his quote from Isaiah, as if waiting for an answer; but as none was forthcoming, beyond a clearing of throats, he continued: 'And to whom is the arm of the Lord revealed?'

Another quiet hush filled the kirk, while those in the gallery could see the gravestones around the building; the budding trees trembling in the cold wind that beat against the window panes, the green fields awakening to the throes and joys of spring-time.

'For he shall grow up before him as a tender plant, as a root out of dry ground,' and some of the farmer cheils remembered their turnip seedlings in a dry season.

Once he had their attention the Rev. Thow brought Christ into the picture: 'He hath no form nor comeliness; and when we shall see him, there is no beauty that we should desire him.

'He is despised and rejected of men; a man of sorrows, and acquainted with grief: and we hid as it were our faces from him; he was despised, and we esteemed him not.

'Surely he hath borne our griefs, and carried our sorrows ... He was wounded for our transgressions ... and with his stripes we are healed.

'All we like sheep have gone astray ...' and just as one old farmer was nodding asleep he suddenly remembered the lambing at home and sat bolt upright.

The Rev. Thow continued: 'We have turned everyone to his own way; and the Lord hath laid on him the iniquity of us all.

'He was oppressed, and he was afflicted, yet he opened not his mouth: he is brought as a lamb to the slaughter, and as a sheep before her shearers is dumb, so he openeth not his mouth.'

Then some old crofter woman remembered her pet lamb on market day and the Rev. Thow had all her sympathy and deepest respect. He didn't believe in flights of fancy but stuck close to the earth, and the good folks of Pittentumb revered him.

The blood of the Saviour was passed round the pews in a big goblet, old men dipping their beards in the wine, the women taking a dainty sip and passing it on from hand to hand, likewise the trenchards of crumbled bread. 'Can you drink of the cup of which I drink?' the Rev. Thow cried out to his congregation, and when nobody spoke in the moment of silence he replied for the disciples to their Master: 'And they said: we can drink!' This was something you had seen on the war memorial to the soldiers of the parish who had died in the war, and you knew that in their case it meant blood. But like Badgie sitting there by you they had not flinched and had drunk their fill. Badgie had survived to tell the tale, and he said he had seen a lot of Christs killed in the war; even crucified in the snows of the Alps on the Italian front, and not much said about it, because you couldn't make a religion out of all their individual sufferings, so we had to have one Christ to atone for all.

After the hymn singing the minister gave his blessing and the benediction, then went to the door to shake hands with everybody as they left. But like the women folk comparing their hats you looked in vain for another suit like your own among all the congregation of Peatriggs. It made you feel terribly conspicuous and you couldn't bear the thought of it a second time; everybody looking you up and down and whispering among themselves like you was a criminal in their midst. Nor could you afford to buy another suit, so you had the Rev. Thow come to the house on some pretence or other, rewarding him with a high tea and home bakes that he enjoyed immensely, and little Brian never swore a word when he was christened and you was thankful for that.

Winifred was born in the spring, a fine healthy eight-pound girl and you left Kingask at the end of May, back to a place in the Bogside. But nowhere could you find comparison for that suit, not even in Brochan, and though everybody said you looked just grand in it you could never quite forget yourself when wearing it; not even in the pictures, and that was saying something. It was well on in the summer, the very first time you had been to Turra Show, where you went in the bus with Kathleen and Brian and little Winifred (Winnie you called her for short) still looking for somebody with a suit like your own. You was beginning to feel something of a martyr and the damned thing had become an obsession; not in any serious sense but as a sort of game, like looking for the last bit of a jig-saw puzzle that had got lost, an awfully important bit, and Kathleen had even joined you in the search, scanning the crowd where you sat on the grass in the Haughs o' Turra, watching the sports. It was the year that Harry Gordon opened the show, the wee Laird of Inversnecky in his kilt and sporran, and steam trains were still arriving at Turriff station, bringing folk from as far afield as Banff and Inveramsay, though Alexanders' buses brought a lot more besides from all over the place, so that the Haughs were thronged with people, and you thought that surely from all that crowd you was bound to find somebody with a suit like yours.

But not among all the thousands of men at Turriff Show did

44

you see one suit like your own, not one. Kathleen pointed out two or three that were quite near it but 'not bright enough', she would say disappointedly, or 'it's a different texture; duller, nae nearly sae noticeable,' and 'na na, that one's nae the same at all!' Out of all the hundreds who came and went on the haughs there was no corresponding suit. So engrossed was you in the search that you missed the parade of farm animals, sparing only a glance at the parade ring while you scanned the crowd. Even the sports were only a sideline though you nearly forgot yourself in the tug-o' war teams, especially the Bells from Tyrie, pulling everything in sight, from Alness to Strathdon, Wartle and Tarland; and all the Heavies were there, George Clark from Grange, Jim Anderson, Norman Murray, A. J. Stuart, tossing the caber, weightlifting, wrestling, throwing the heavy hammer (though Harry Gordon said it was the heavy bag-pipes) and such was the cheering at these events, and great surge of enthusiasm among the spectators that you got completely carried away, forgetting all about your daft suit till Kathleen gave you a nudge with her elbow and directed your gaze in the other direction. And there she was, not more than two feet from your right-hand side, a fine young girl in a costume suit exactly like your own. She must have come down the terrace from the back, for even Kathleen never saw her approach, not until she sat down beside you where someone had left a vacant seat. Well, well, that was it; the end of your search for the missing piece of jig-saw, the culmination of your obsession, though you had never expected a woman to solve your problem. Had she done it on purpose? Both of you looked at her but she pretended not to notice. Kathleen looked at you in a half-smile and you winked back at her, message understood. But somehow the suit looked fine on the girl; maybe a woman wouldn't look so bad with a suit like that in church – or anywhere, she was so nice. If you looked half as well in the same outfit you had nothing to worry about.

But could you let her go without saying a word? Never in this world were you ever likely to see her again and it was so funny. You knew nothing about her: where she came from, nothing. And being a married man it was none of your business. The kids were getting restless and soon you would have to go. You whispered your thoughts to Kathleen and she agreed you should speak to the quine: ask if she had spied you out in the crowd and had sat beside you on purpose? But you was so shy. It was such a silly thing to ask anybody; especially with your wife and kids sitting beside you ... maybe a bit different if you had been a single body. It was on the tip of your tongue several times but you just couldn't say it. It was so embarrassing. It was just as awkward for Kathleen and she wouldn't say anything either. Maybe the quine would think she was being accused of trying to flirt with you. And anyway Kathleen was preoccupied changing Winnie's wet nappie. You tried to catch the lassie's attention by just looking at her, without any positive approach, watching her face, but she averted her eyes and looked at the sports, smiling rather shyly when something pleased her. You felt sure she stole a glance at you when you was whispering to Kathleen. You could almost feel her soft pleading eyes on your back, on the colour of your suit – but when you turned round quickly she looked away again. Perhaps she was feeling as you had felt; shunned and neglected, wanting to say something, she knew not what nor how. Strange that she didn't have a lad with her, a pretty girl like that. How long had she searched for you and how far? Maybe she had detested her costume and couldn't afford another one? Perhaps she had used it to attract your attention, by sitting down beside you – until she discovered that you was not alone, that Kathleen was your wife. How was she to know really among all the crowd? Maybe the whole damned thing was just plain coincidence – though not likely, not among all the thousands of folk at Turra Show and only two of you dressed alike; birds of a feather and you had sought each other.

But now you were going. You had to get your supper before bus time, up in one of the restaurants in the town. You were on your feet but the girl still sat there, merely giving you a glance when you stood up, a little forlorn like you thought but maybe it was just your imagination. You took Brian in your arms and followed Kathleen down the hill, Winnie in her oxter, now fast asleep. When you glanced back the lassie was still sitting there, her hat tilted slightly on the back of her head, now staring after you, watching you all the way down the brae, and you could still pick her out from the sports ring when you reached the bottom. You would remember that colour anywhere, wherever you saw it again – but you never did. Once was enough and you was satisfied. Yes she was still sitting there, still watching you – such a pity you hadn't spoken to her after all.

But you wore that suit for years after that; even for Sunday until you could afford another one, cottar brown next time so that you could go to the kirk somewhere for the christening of Winnie. But whenever you felt abashed in your loud checked suit you just remembered that lonely quine sitting there in the Haughs o' Turra; for at least there was one other person in the whole wide world who had a costume suit exactly the same as your own.

And if you had been a film director you might have signed her up on contract, even without a screen test, because of her loud checked suit and the satisfaction it had given you.

Hardwood!

The fog being down on the countraside when you couldna see a stirk in your ain parks in broad daylight was the time that Hardwood Harry choose to disappear. Harry Hernie was an old widower who had lived with his twin son and dother on the fairm of Clayfoons since his wife died, which was as many years back that younger folks couldna mind on't. Harry had been a joiner and undertaker in his younger day, before he took over the fairm from his father, and when his own turn came for growing old he handed over the lease to his unmarried twins, Wattie and Bannie Hernie, who had been born at Clayfoons and lived and worked there all their days, and were well on in middle-age when their father handed over the place to them.

But when the old man retired he had a hankering to go back to his joinery, or maybe it was just that he couldna rest and content himself in idleness, and there wasn't all that wark for him on a pair place of sixty acres, for Wattie and Bannie did most of it, so he started making barrows for the farming folk round about Clayfoons, lightsome kind of wark making box-barrows for mucking out their byres and stables, and lighter, flat-leaf barrows for wheeling out their peat in summer, peat barrows with a broader wheel for the soft lairs. Hardwood became a dab hand at the barrows, and they were that well made with good seasoned wood and lasted such a long time that they carried his name all over the district, and if you didn't have a Hardwood barrow sitting on your midden plank you just wasn't worth speaking to.

Hardwood had built a fairly big shed at the gable of the stead-
ng, near the peat stack, and set up a bench in it with a vice, and a
~ along the wall for all the hand tools he needed for making
~airing barrows, besides a small circular base outside where
~ the iron rings when he fitted them on the wheels, kindl-
~ith peat like the blacksmith did with the heavier cart

wheels. The box-barrows he painted blue, with red inside and wheel, the peat barrows a dull brown, so they had a fine smell of fresh paint about them when you went in by with a horse cart for one of Hardwood's barrows.

Trade was brisk, because there was a lot of knacky work in making a farm barrow, and there weren't many joiners who took the trouble, so Hardwood got steady work to meet the demand for barrows. By and by he was earning more bawbees from his barrow making than his son was doing on the farm, so that a bit of jealousy sprang up between Wattie and his father, and even Bannie took sides with her brother against the old man, which wasn't surprising maybe them being twins. And sometimes Bannie kept the money when honest folk came to pay their accounts and there was a fair din about the place when the old man found her out. Hardwood would charge the customer a second time and when the body told him he had already paid his dother at the back kitchie door the old man was dumfoonert that his ain flesh and bleed could treat him like this. So he kept the books himself and told his customers to pay him in the shed, 'to keep things right', as he said, though folk kent fine what Bannie was up to, and they thought it a right shame to swick the old man.

But he ups and gives Bannie and Wattie a right tinking with his sharp tongue and says they wouldna have done that gin their mother had been alive, poor soul, for it was enough to make her topple the stone that held her down in the kirkyard at the Bog-side, and them huggin' and kissin' at one another, what would she think of that? Oh aye, he'd seen them at it he said, he wasn't blind or very deaf, and it wasn't a way for a brother and sister to be carrying on, even though they were twins. And what did they want with his money anyway? Wouldn't they get it all when he was dead and away, and they already had the lease of the place; but if they didn't mend their ways he would wipe them out of his will and leave every penny to others more deserving that he could think of.

But this outburst had little effect on the twins, in fact it made them worse when they knew that their relationship had been dis-covered; so they plotted and planned between them to make the old man's life a misery. So Bannie scrimps her old father at the table and treats him like a tike at the door, so that he could hardly light his pipe in the kitchen, living on kale brose like a cater-pillar on a cabbage runt. So the old man took to sleeping on a couch in his joinery shed, covered up with rugs and old jackets, and kept himself warm with a bit peek of a stove that he burned with wood shavings and sawdust and broken peat, till he was nearly smoared with the reek, and his old brown eyes like to run out of his head, and when customers found him like this the twins at Clayfoons became the claik of the Buchan howes.

Folk that were ill-mannered and spied in at the window after dark said that Wattie Hernie and his sister both slept in the same bed, and that they kissed and cuddled at each other like they were man and wife, and were likely to be doing most other things besides, though nothing had come of it and maybe they were just lucky. And they said that this annoyed the old man more than his ill-usage or taking his money, for he knew fine what was going on and that was why he had taken to sleeping on his couch in the joinery shed, maybe to spite them and set the neighbours talking, which might arouse a little sympathy for himself or bring the twins to their senses. But there were others who said plainly that the twins had shut their old father out of the farmhouse so that he couldn't spy on their courting, and that it was what the old fool deserved for giving them the farm in the first place.

Och but they said everything but their prayers in the Bogside, and Bannie Hernie didn't seem to care that much what they said, or maybe she just got used to their wagging tongues; so the old man lay on his couch till his hurdies were sore and the rheuma-tism stiffened him, and what with the want of proper food for his belly he became as thin and unwashed as a starved tink and fit to scare the craws from your tattie dreels. Fell crabbit he was too in nis old age and like to bite off your lug of a morning when you went in by with a barrow wheel that needed to be fitted with a new iron ring on it for a tyre. And if you hadn't given it a dabble in the mill-dam to wash off all the sharn you heard about it from old Hardwood, which was odd you thought when he was sorer in need of a scrub himself, and folk thought he was getting a bit dottled in his old age, though he still had a waspish tongue.

But he wasn't as dottled as they thought the stock, for after his day at the barrow making old Hardwood began working at something in the evening, so that if you went past Clayfoons in the dark on your bicycle you'd see a light in the far end of Hardwood's shed and the old man plaining and chiseling or spokeshaving at something in the lamplight, so that though you got off your bike and went to the window for a peep you still couldn't make out what he was working at; maybe just another barrow you thought, and that he couldn't cope with the demand, and though you made an errand in by in daylight he always had the thing covered up, longish in shape it was, like a boat, though you didn't like to ask lest he told you to mind your own business, for he could be snappish at times.

Then Hardwood locked his shed and disappeared into the fog that had been hanging about for days on the hairst parks, so that you couldn't see the lads at stook parade, and the fog-horn at the Battery Head moaning all day and night like a cow foonert at the calving. When her father didn't go in for breakfast Bannie went over to the shed to waken him. She tried the lock and hammered on the door but when there was no response to her knocking she looked in the window. He wasn't in his couch either so she went to the far end and looked in the other window. The light was coming in slowly but she saw the naked coffin on its trestles, uncovered now for anyone who cared to look at it, and Bannie got a sore fright, for there it stood in polished oak, with brass handles on the ends and black cords and toshels draped along its sides, with a lid on top. Bannie couldn't think of anyone who had ordered a coffin from her father, nor could she mind of a new death in the Bogside, or anybody like to die that would be needing one, and it was the first coffin she had seen the old man make in his retirement, though she knew he had been an undertaker in his younger day.

Bannie tried the door again but it wouldn't budge, so she walked round the shed and came back to the window where the coffin was, staring in at it until she had a daft idea that her father must have made it for himself, that he would be lying in there now, and she rapped on the window with her knuckles, hoping to waken him up, half expecting the lid to be raised and the old man look out at her in his working clothes, reminding her of her illtreatment and making her promise to mend her ways with her twin brother. Guilt began to rankle in Bannie's mind and she promised herself that though the old man was only playing a joke on her she would mend her ways, and the hot tears came into her eyes and she hammered on the window till it shook and cried out 'Father, oh father, speak to me. I promise father, I promise . . .' and the greet grew loud in her throat, until you could hear it across the road, and the tears ran down her face and the dog came barking round and then Wattie to see what ailed his sister, thinking maybe that somebody had ravished her at the back of the shed.

Wattie took Bannie in his oxter but she thrust him aside, pointing at the coffin through the window. 'Father's missing,' she cried, 'and I'll swear he's in there now, waiting for us to promise something. All the time we've been wicked he's been watching and this is our last chance. We must promise never to do it again Wattie!' She was sobbing hard and Wattie said 'promise nothing' and pressed his nose against the glass, shading the growing light with his open hands against his cheeks, and when he saw the gleaming coffin on its trestles he was sore taken aback. 'So that was what he was hammerin' at in the evenin's. It's a pity Bannie that we didna take a look over to see what he was at. I juist thocht it was anither barra.'

'I'll go to the hoose and see if I can find anither key,' Bannie said, a bit calmed down since Wattie came round, but she could find no other key to the shed. Wattie shook the door by the knob but it wouldn't move, so he threw his weight against it and burst it open, near going head first after it into the shed. Bannie followed him past the couch and the bench, the floor deep in wood shavings and a fine smell of wood and rosin and paint, with half-finished barrows propped against the walls and wheels on the floor, bits of sawn wood, sawdust and nails, and the coffin at the far end. The twins stood beside it, afraid to open the lid, like bairns with a Jack-in-the-Box, afraid that when they opened the lid their father would leap up in their faces and cry 'Bah!' A sudden frightening shout that would scare them to fits; or he would be lying in there asleep or dead, white and cold as snow and would never speak to them again in this world.

'You open it Bannie. I did my bit bursting the door.'

'No I couldna, and what if he is in there listening to us arguing aboot wha will open his coffin lid.' And Bannie was near to tears again.

Wattie plucked up courage and prised his thick thumbs under the heavy lid, until he got his hand under it and lifted it up on its edge, holding it there, wide open, while the two of them stared into the empty coffin, lined with white cotton, and Bannie couldn't think where her father had gotten all this stuff, unless he had ordered it through the post.

But the old man was not in the coffin, nor hiding in the shed, or anywhere about the steading or the farmhouse, for they had searched high and low for him, though Bannie was sure the coffin was a sign or a warning that they would find him dead some-where. So they searched all the burns and hedges on Clayfoons and crawled under all the stooks on the hairst rigs looking for him, or simply threw them down in despair, hoping that they would find their father asleep somewhere and nobody would know about his disappearance, and they would be kinder to him after this scare, for he had certainly given them a lesson and they wouldn't forget it.

But no old man leapt out at them from any stook, and he had disappeared at a time that would give them plenty to think about, this misty season in the middle o' hairst when he would be ill to find, and when most other folks would have other things on their minds, what with their uncut corn drooping and weeping in the seep of the rain and the stubble as wet you could hardly set a stook on it, the burns all in spate and the snipes wheebling in the segs, though you couldna see them for the fog.

Before the day was out Bannie had to run up to Whistlebrae and tell them what had happened, and would they telephone the bobbies to come and help them look for her father. A sore dis-grace it would be to the pair of them, but things had reached a stage when they felt they would be worse guilty if they didn't report it.

For two whole days half the countraside searched for the mis-sing joiner, in the burns and hedges, in the segs and on the braes, among the whin and broom around the quarries, and up among the fir trees on the Spionkop, the highest hill in the Bogside. Folk even drained their mill-dams, thinking old Hardwood would stick in the sluice or go down the lade, but there was never a sign of him, not even in the miller's dam. The polis looked everywhere they could think of, and even the school bairns were told to look out for the old man when they went over the moors and through the woods.

The stone quarry at Spionkop was a deep hole of water on the face of the brae, and the polis got a fire-engine out of the toon with long hoses that went over the grass from the road and sucked the quarry dry, but the firemen shook their helmeted heads when they came upon all the rubbish at the bottom of the quarry but no sign of Hardwood. Folk wondered about the moss pots filled with brown peaty water that had no bottom to them, where a body might sink far enough and never be seen again, and they shuddered at the thought. Lads on stook parade in the hairst parks expected to find old Hardwood in every stook they shifted, and when you thought of all the multitude of corn and barley stooks in the Laich o' Buchan where an old body could hide you knew fine the old man wasn't a dottard; that he had chosen the right time to keep folk on the move, especially the twins at Clayfoons, for they hadna stickit an eye since he went missing.

Now you couldn't see the hill of the Spionkop from Clayfoons, though it was but two miles as the crow flies. You couldn't see it for the strip of wood on the Berry-hill, even though the cottars had thinned it with their axes over the years; beyond was the moss and the segs and the grass parks that lay on the shin of the Spionkop. It was an unco name to give a bit hill and you thought maybe it was that if you went up there on a fine day you could spy on the folk in the howe; but it took its name from the farmtoon high on its slopes, where a Dutch chiel from South Africa had bought the place, and being home-sick he changed the name from Fellrigs to Spionkop, and some said he was a Boer, seeing his name was Vanderskelp or something. But since he came to live there on the face of the brae they called it the Spionkop, which well-read folk told you was somewhere in Natal, and had something to do with a battle that the British had out there with the Boers, those ill-mannered chiels that were but farming folk and shot at the British like they were hares in the parks. But maybe the Vanderskelp chiel meant no harm, because the Boers got a thrashing at the Spionkop, and yon General Buller had to run with his breeks down, so maybe the lad was giving you credit naming your Buchan hill after a Boer defeat. Anyway the fus-

54

kered postie said that was the new address, and when you thought of other places in Buchan with foreign names like Waterloo, Pisgah and Jericho you wasn't surprised. And the postie said the Boer was a right civil chiel to speak to and that he didn't have a barking dog that would tear the arse out of your breeks like some he knew in the Bogside.

You had gone up on the Spionkop yourself in your time, looking for a Druids' Circle in such a likely place, but not a lintel stone did you find there from the olden days, nor any sign of a fort, for the Buchan Howes had small protection from the Vikings when the horned chiels came over in their long-boats from the Norse Lands, though King Malcolm had licked the Danes at Cruden Bay, and you could still see the cairns that marked their graves at Cairncatto, and such a song of the curlew there it was like an eternal requiem for the dead in their long forgotten burrows.

But down at the foot of the Spionkop lived Maggie Lawrence in her thachet biggin', where the fuschias hung their ruby bells over the stone dyke the long summer through, and the dog-rose clung to the walls, while the smell of dewy honeysuckle on an evening clear would nearly sicken you with pleasure, like you had drunk too much wine for your stomach's sake. Maggie was an old toothless body that could neither read nor write, and she lived there alone but for the rats that fed with her at table, and if you looked through her peep-hole windows with the little lace curtains you'd see old Maggie with her pets, and if any one of the creatures was impatient enough to snatch a morsel from Maggie she would give it a right quick smack with her hazel stick and cry out: 'Get doon ye Ted!' And the long-tailed rat would slink away to the other end of the table, with great respect for Maggie when her ire was up. When Maggie died your grandfather had to sit up with her corpse at night to keep the rats away from her coffin, and right glad he was when the funeral was over because he was afraid of the brutes.

But meanwhile Maggie was still very much alive, smoking her clay pipe and gathering whin sticks on the brae for her fire, and any of the divots that she could rive from the heather. She carried her water from a wee well on the edge of a grass park just beyond her door, and Maggie would put on her bit plaid of red tartan with the tassled edges and a yoke on her shoulders, with two galvanized pails hanging from it, her clay pipe in her mooth, the blue reek taking over her canty shoulder, away to the well for her drop water.

It was but two or three feet deep Maggie's well, a tender spring out of the sand with a trout in it to keep the water clean, and sometimes a frog that lept in to keep him company, and whiles a shrew-mouse that fell in by mistake, swam itself to exhaustion and drowned, and was thrown out by Maggie when she caught it in her pail. Maggie spoke to her trout like he was a human body, and they said he cocked an eye at her when her reflection hit the water. So it was a great surprise to her that day when she found this great big trout in her well, soon as she opened the gate that was for keeping out the cattle beasts, for here was this man standing in her well up to his thighs, his back bent level with the ground, his white head jammed into the water so that he couldn't fall over, his body supported by the rim of the wall. Old Hardwood at last, where nobody thought to look for him, drowned in Maggie's well. She dropped her pails and took the wooden yoke from her neck, stuck her bit pipe in the pocket of her apron and wondered where she would go for help. But first she went a bit closer to the human statue, crouched with its feet and hands in the well, bent in supplication the creature seemed, praying for death with its mouth in the water. Maggie went down the step and put her hand on the cold stiff shoulder, like a stuffed thing, swelling inside the damp clothing. She knew he was dead but she wasn't afraid of the poor old man, just wondered how he came to be there, and how she would ever have the heart again to drink the crystal clear water from her wallie. A pity she couldna see his face to see who he might be, for she knew nothing of Hardwood's disappearance, though she kenned that sic a body lived in the Bogside. His jacket pockets were bulging in the water and Maggie lifted the sodden flap to see what might be in there, thinking maybe it was bawbees, though it didn't seem likely when he had done away with himself, or so she supposed, for nobody could put an old man into a well like that without a struggle, and he was as composed and peaceful as a sleeping lamb; not a speck of blood on him, nor a tare in his jacket, not a hair of his head ravelled and nothing in the well, nothing but the trootie, straight as an eel in the bottom. His jacket pockets were stuffed with coiryarn, coconut-hair rope that the farmer chiels were using nowadays to hold down their rucks and strae-soos, instead of straw rape, and Maggie thought the poor creature had been fell determined to put an end to himself, and that if the drowning failed he would hang himself from a fir tree on the Spionkop.

The fog had cleared and Maggie warsled away up the hill to Mr Vanderskelp, who was kind of a landlord to her, 'cause her clay biggin' was on his grun, though he never charged her any rent for the sagging roofed venel that she lived in, little more than a cairn of stones and clay with one lum and an earthen floor, a hallan that some crofter chiel had biggit for his family a hunder years agone, with stones gathered on the hillside.

Mr Vanderskelp heard Maggie's story and said he had been through the park counting his cattle that very morning but never thought of looking in the well. It seemed impossible that anyone could drown himself in such a shallow trough. Maggie would have called it a wee skite of water, but never mind, she knew fine what he meant and she agreed with her laird. Mr Vanderskelp then telephoned the bobby and told him to get the doctor, and they came and lifted the dripping Hardwood out of Maggie's well and laid him on the yird, all but his false teeth that they found later and Maggie hadn't seen, and maybe just as well, for it might have scunnered her completely from taking water there.

Two of Mr Vanderskelp's men lifted the corpse on to a spring-cart and took him to Clayfoons, the water still dripping out of the cart, and followed by the school bairns that were on their way home at the time. So the undertaker came in his black coat and stretched out Hardwood on a board and shaved him and laid him in his home-made coffin in the ben room. And Bannie bibbled and grat over him like a long lost bairn and would hardly bide in the hoose without a neighbour woman for company or the funeral was by. And such a trail of a funeral that the likes of it had never been seen in the Bogside, the road fair jammed with phaetons and gigs and Governess cars with their shelts and ponies and a motor car or twa, and the kirkyard black with folk, like the craws after a thrashin' mull, and Wattie Hernie by the gate when they left, shakin' as mony hands ye would have thought he was ca'in' a pump, with saut tears hingin' at his mouser.

So that was Hardwood and his barrows, and they survived him for mony a year and day, keeping his memory green in the Bogside, green as the sod where he lay with his wife at the gable o' the kirk yonder. But the twins didn't stay long in the fairm after this, maybe because they had a guilty conscience, though the neighbours gave them no cause to feel it. They had a roup the two of them the next May and sold nearly everything but the furniture and the grandfather clock. Everything else went: horse, nowt, pigs and poultry; pleuchs, harrows, grubber and rollers; binder, mower, scythes and horse-rake, all the hand tools and two or three of Hardwood's barrows and wheels that gave a stunning price. Sic a steer there was and a day or two after this the twins got a stem-waggon and lifted all their gear and set sail out of the Bogside and that was the last you ever heard of them.

The Souter

All through the first summer at Kingask, the place you was cottared at, and through the long winter evenings of your spare time, and now into spring, you had laboured at the Queen Mary – nine precious months you had expended on this labour of love to create a model ship that was the cardboard image (or very near it) of the famous Queen of Clydebank, a queer hobby for a fairm body and folk just thought you was a bit daft.

You got your cardboard in the village, down in Candlebay there by the sea, and most of it from Jimmie Duthie the souter, who gave you spare shoeboxes when a customer didn't want them. He also gave you two sheets of tough hardened leather three feet by fifteen inches to make the hull, which cost you nearly a fortnight's wages, and thread waxed with rosin to stitch it together. Jimmie had been a pal of yours almost from the first month you came to Kingask, when you had gone down to have your Sunday shoes soled, and a pair of Kathleen's that needed the heels built up, and Jimmie Duthie had made such a good job of it and had charged so little that you always went back. There was another shoemaker in the village called Tackie Broon, because he tacked his trousers to his wooden leg to scare the bairns when they annoyed his budgerigars. Tackie had lost his leg in the war but he said he still had cold feet from standing so long in the wet trenches. He kept budgerigars in cages all round the shop, the chorus of birds all chirping away while he hammered in the tackets on a last between his knees, sitting on a wooden chair as natural like that until he stood up you would never have noticed that he had a wooden leg. Tackie Broon had done well for a time and was awfully popular with the bairns, who came in by after school to see his birds, and to listen to their chirping in the cages. But Tackie Broon wasn't all that fond of bairns, nor did he have any of his own, though he was married, and his wife came through from ben the hoose occasionally to feed the budgies and clean out their cages and tidy the shop. But the bairns were a bit of a nuisance to Tackie Broon and he felt they were upsetting his aviary, the birds dashing themselves against the wire meshes, until he devised a way to get rid of the bairns; so he started driving the tackets through his breeks into his wooden leg and this fair frightened them, especially the younger offenders, who couldn't understand about the wooden leg. It kept the bairns away for months but he lost trade over it, because the bairns took their parents' shoes for repair to Jimmie Duthie, who was a bachelor and genuinely fond of the bairns, but was now swamped under the load of work they brought him, hammering away in his back shop while his sister brought him jugs of hot strong tea to keep him going at his last.

So like the bairns you didn't bother Tackie Broon very much, because he was a bit surly at the best of times, so you became great friends with souter Duthie, and after a whilies newsing together he learned of your daftness about boats and the sea, and when he learned you was also a reader he gave you books like Southey's *Life of Nelson*; *Buccaneers of the Pacific* and *The Riddle of Jutland*, all of which you devoured with relish, and when you told him about your hobby, and your cherished ambition to build a model of the Queen Mary, which had just been launched on the Clyde, he gave you all the strongest cardboard you required and shoe-wax to seal your stitching and to make it water-tight along the three-foot length of keel. Jimmie added that his father had been a great reader, and so was his sister, and that the house was stacked with books, so if ever you wanted a book just come in by.

The first thing you did was to make a wooden platform with notches to hold the keel, so that the giant ship wouldn't topple over, because you wouldn't have room to work with side supports. Then you shaped the hull, first with a yacht bow, both sides exactly the same; cut out the port holes with a sharp knife, then stitched the two sides together with Jimmie Duthie's thread, using an awl to punch the rivet holes, the glossy surface of the leather outmost for painting, and to make the ship water-tight, pouring hot wax into the seams. The walls of the giant hull were now prised apart and straddled with double deck supports fixed with sprigs or small nails, forcing out the bilges to the shape required and pulling in the yacht bow to a shorter angle, then filling with cement to keep the shape and reinforce the hull, judging the correct amount to serve as ballast, though more weight could be added with pebbles through the holds when launching the ship. You had cut the hull walls with a slightly upward curve in the middle, arching from bow to stern, so that when pulled apart they were now level for laying the deck, fitting masts and funnels, building the bridge and cabins, tasks that are usually completed in the fitting-out basin after launching, but in this case would have to be done beforehand, because you couldn't really guess the weight of your superstructure, which would have to be corrected with the final ballast.

During the launching of the real Queen you had cut out all the photographs from the papers and weekly magazines and these you studied in great detail, even closer now that actual building had begun, though you wasn't going to do it to scale, rather using your own judgement in the size of things, which you thought would be good experience when you turned to scale building with some future models.

The Queen Mary now occupied the whole of the kitchen table, when Kathleen had cleared everything away to let you work, meanwhile gazing at this monstrosity you was making; something she had never seen her brothers at, them being country loons and more interested in ploughing and horses. Maybe it was the time in your boyhood you had lived in the town that had drawn your attention to ships, when you was always at the harbour after school hours; the harbour or the railway station, which were linked by a single set of rails for coaling the herring drifters. Now at Kingask by the sea you were trying to recapture this early influence; to express it in art form, though other folk might say you hadn't grown up properly and was still a loon at heart, which wasn't a bad thing really when you came to think about it.

At table-leaf level your Queen was a magnificent ship, her graceful, forward sweeping bow towering above the teacups at bedtime, her long sleek sides and decks stretching to her stern at the other end of the table, awaiting a rudder and propellers in the normal method of ship construction. When work was in progress Kathleen had to guard the Queen with her life almost; guard it against little Brian, your small son, whose fingers were just now reaching the table, and at bed-time every night the liner was carried upstairs out of his reach next day.

It took a whole evening to make one cardboard funnel, about the size of a modern beer tin (which would have served the purpose then – had it been invented) papered over to hold it together (before the days of sellotape) a flat disc inside to keep the shape, then slipped into the hole shaped for it in the upperstructure behind the bridge. It took about the same time to make an air vent; two evenings to construct a lifeboat complete with ratlines and tarpaulin covers, rudder and propeller, and even oars in case of engine failure; and as there were three funnels, six engine-room vents and a dozen lifeboats (though the real Queen had twenty-four) a body gets some idea of the time and patience spent on the upperstructure, prior to launching in this case; including the bridgework, sweeping out over the side of the hull, and the actual wheelhouse and control room, tennis courts, swimming pool and railings (using gramophone needles) linked with white thread, masts and companion ways, and as the new polythene paper had just made its appearance you used this for glass in the portholes and cabin windows. It was the most wonderful thing to date you had ever made in your life and strangers in the house gazed at it in wonder. Its great size captured everybody's imagination from the start, though a closer study by experts would have revealed your lack of scaling, but quite proportionate in every detail, down to the anchors and cap-stans on the foredeck, which was scored with pencil to simulate boarding – rope ladders, shrouds, wireless aerial, stairways and crow's nest.

The final painting was done with Japlac, black enamel gloss for the upper part of the hull, red keel to the bilges, with a white stripe for the waterline and plimsoll markings; varnished decks and masts, white cabins and lifeboats, black funnels with red tops and a white stripe between red propellers and rudder, with tufts of white cottonwool in the funnels.

During construction of the 'Queen' your kitchen was a minia-ture John Brown's shipyard, except for the towering derricks and the hammering of rivet guns; everything in a muddle for the final achievement, and there were even strikes and suspension of work when you was too tired or just not in the mood to go on, but after an evening or two in your armchair you was back on the job again. Cunard halted work on the real Queen Mary for lack of capital in the hungry' thirties. The great ship was abandoned for nearly two years and unemployment soared on the Clyde. Eventually the Government provided funds and work was resumed on the skeleton hull. The gesture was more to ease distress than to finish the luxury liner, though the final result is unparalleled in maritime achievement.

But before the launching in the miller's dam you thought that Badgie Summers the foreman next door should see your masterpiece. His daughter Esma had looked at it several times during construction when she had come round for little Brian. Mrs Summers had stared at it with folded arms over the kitchen table and said you was at the wrong job feeding nowt and pulling turnips when you was so good with your hands. Most likely they had told Badgie of your accomplishment but so far he had never seen it. So one fine Sunday morning after byre time, after you'd had your tea and a smoke, you went upstairs for your 'Queen' and set her on the kitchen table. She really was a magnificent sight, the fresh smelling enamel gloss gleaming in the morning sunshine, perfect almost in every detail, even to the guy-ropes of black thread holding the masts, all ready for launching.

You told Kathleen that you wanted to show the foreman your boat, because you felt so proud of it, but she said you shouldn't bother because most likely he would only laugh at you; that you knew fine he hadn't much time for such capers, nothing in his mind but his work, and that he never even troubled himself to put soles on his family's shoes (as her own father had done with their large family) but sat in his corner chair all evening and left it to Tackie Broon the shoemaker. No, Kathleen said, Badgie had no time for hobbies other than his work and wouldn't likely be interested. All the same you took the great ship in your arms and went down the close to Badgie, rested the 'Queen' on your knee and knocked on the door with your free hand, and when Esma opened it you walked in and set Queen Mary on the table by the window. Badgie and the blacksmith were seated in armchairs on each side of the fire, Badgie nearest the window, where he leaned round to gaze at your handiwork. The blacksmith glowered with mild interest across the kitchen, but neither of them rose to give your ship a closer inspection, while you stood in the middle of the floor like an overgrown schoolboy showing off a fabulous new toy, the only difference being that you had made the thing yourself.

'Aye faith,' says Badgie, trying his best to be complimentary: 'Some wark gaen intae that thing. It's a wonder ye have the patience. It's mair than I could dae onywye.'

Badgie's wife sat apart, admiring the model from afar, as if it were in Candlebay harbour and she was feared to go near the water. 'A bonnie piece o' work,' she said, 'I dinna ken fut wye ye can be bothered; but I suppose it's fine for takin' up yer attention in the winter evenin's.'

Finally the blacksmith offered his criterion: 'But that thing wunna put onything in ye pooch man; there's nae bawbees tae be made at that kind o' wark!'

Your answer to that remark would have been that if you was going to spend most of it in the pub like he did it didn't matter, but of course you didn't want to be cheeky; and after all none of them had asked you round to show off your boat. But you was showing them a piece of intricate art contrived by serious study and concentration and all they could think about was money – how much you could get out of it materially – without a thought for the satisfaction of your achievement and the many happy hours it had given you. So you just lifted your boat from the table and politely left the house, wondering what the blacksmith had said after you left. 'A queer lad' (most likely) 'makin' boats: naething tae be made at that!' But most likely Badgie would stick up for you: 'Aye but he's a' there though, more than the spoon puts in; a sober stock maybe but he can cairry a bag o' corn up the laft stair wi' the neist ane – and he's nae a feel either!'

Kathleen asked what they thought about your boat, and you said 'Oh, not very much; a waste of time showing it to them – they're nae interested in boats, naething in their heids but money.'

'No,' she replied, 'they wouldna understand ye as I do, though it tak's me a' my time whiles the things ye get up tae.'

The launching in the miller's dam was perfect, with just the right amount of ballast to keep the ship afloat, swinging slightly in the breeze, so that you didn't have to open the hatches to add more pebbles. She was strung with flags between the masts, with a Union Jack on the stern, and a string from the bows to your hand on the dam bank, where you guided her over the ripples, her stately bow dipping slightly over the waterline. Some of the village loons came up to watch your one-ship regatta; seeing there wasn't a yachting pond in the village, nothing but the harbour, with its patches of oil and barrel staves floating at the pier. So you asked one of the loons if he would go and get hold of Jimmie Duthie the shoemaker, seeing that he had provided the material, and when he saw the Queen Mary afloat on the miller's dam he hailed you with 'Hey there! Anchors ahoy! All hands on deck!' But we didn't break a bottle over her bows, which would have been like hitting the *Titanic* with the iceberg.

Jimmie Duthie was the most amazing shoemaker you had ever seen, hammering away in his wee back shop with a mountain of boots and shoes of all descriptions piled on the floor, some of them without name or number, and when Jimmie threw your pair on the heap you felt you could never be sure you would get your own boots back again. But James Duthie Shoemaker (as on the board above the door, his father's name) knew everybody's footwear in the village of Candlebay and half the parish of Pitten-tumb (except for those who went to Tackie Broon) from the costly shoes of the mistress of Kingask to the cheaper mail-order variety on the feet of the kitchiedeem at Fleamiddens, including the bairns of the parish; though some of his customers put a label on their boots and tied the pairs together in case they got lost in Jimmie's back shop, and some of the most mindful of them tucked a pound or a ten-shilling note in the toe of a shoe, hoping that Jimmie would find it when he put the shoe on the last, because he hadn't charged for the previous repair, or sent an account for it.

Over the years the dusty heap of boots and shoes in Jimmie's back shop seemed to get bigger and bigger; never smaller, and now nearly counter high, and you sometimes wondered if he had ever been at the bottom of it; sharny boots and muddy boots, boots that Jimmie would have to scrape and clean before he ever got a start to repair them, just as the cattlemen had left the byre with them, or the ploughman the furrow. The wooden floor was also shovel deep in leather cuttings, shoe nails, iron heel and toe-pieces, discarded protectors, studs, tackets, sprigs, broken boot-laces, and the cigarette packets, match boxes, fag ends and matches thrown down by his various customers. Why Jimmie Duthie's shop wasn't burned down during the night you couldn't imagine (or even during the day) because there was only one ash-tray, the lid of a boot black tin, over by Jimmy's bench, always heaped up and running over, and when the place was crowded and the lads couldn't get near it, they just heeled their tabbies into the years of leather cuttings on the floor, and some of them landed inside a shoe and were left to smoulder. Folk said that Jimmie needed a wife to tidy up his shop, that his sister wasn't able for it, but both were in celibacy and likely to remain so. Lizzie Duthie was such a frail sickly lass that the lads never bothered her, white faced and frizzy headed and slightly bent in the back, with a small lump between her shoulder blades. Jimmie never had a lass they said, though he teased at the quines who came into his shop, servant lassies and the like, though he was far too shy to go the length of kissing them, and if they had taken the initiative most likely he would have sprinted through to his sister in the kitchen. His only relaxation was his weekly game of indoor bowling and shuttlecock in the Masonic Hall in Brochan on Wednesdays, when his shop was closed all day, and if he was a member of the Masonic fraternity he never mentioned the fact.

Down at Tackie Broon's, at the other end of the village, things were much more orderly, even though Tackie had bother getting out of his chair, because his wife looked after the place. You laid your boots on the counter and pulled a string that rang a bell in the kitchen, when Tackie's wife came through and labelled your boots and set them on a rack beside her husband's chair; entered your boots in a ledger with your name and address and told you when to come back for them.

But Tackie Broon had his frailties too. The want of his leg was an affliction that troubled him sorely and sometimes drove him to drink. On occasions he wanted to forget the static, hum-drum world into which his affliction had thrust him. But for months on end he wouldn't touch liquor; *the drink*; his hammer flying from the last with the rhythm of a conductor's baton, while he cupped a handful of sprigs and threw them into his mouth, humming a tune like 'Tipperary', or 'Pack up your troubles in your old kit-bag', broken at intervals while he took a sprig from between his teeth and hammered it into a shoe.

At other times Tackie Broon's eyes had the appearance of a gathering thunderstorm, when he would rise up from his chair, cast aside his chamois leather apron, get into his jacket and hirple down the road to the Spittoon Bar, where he really made a night of it, and some of his old cronies had to carry him home from the pub. Next day his wife would put a notice in the window: NO REPAIRS MEANTIME, and never unlocked the shop door. But after a day or two to recuperate *and* Tackie was back at his last again; happy and contented, fumbling in his tins for hobnails, his right thumb smooth and scored from long years as a buffer for the keen-edged knife slicing through the leather.

When the war came Tackie was scared of the bombing. He had nightmares about lying on his back in a deep trench, the Germans in their steel helmets and fixed bayonets leaping down on him, landing on his chest, stamping his heart into his throat until he gasped with palpitation, and he couldn't get up because of his wounded leg, the blood seeping through his kilt. He gasped himself into consciousness and his wife would be comforting him, smoothing what grey hairs remained on his throbbing temples. He wanted to shout, to scream, to run away from it all; then buried his head in his wife's bosom, while she swabbed away his tears.

But Lizzie Duthie wasn't able to help her brother to this extent, and since their mother died things had gone from bad to worse with them. But she managed to cook his meals for him and do his washing, go for messages and send out his accounts when Jimmie remembered to tell her who had been in the shop. Jimmie never wrote anything down, relying entirely upon memory for all his customers, and those he remembered filtered through to his sister's ledger, and those he forgot were those who left money in their shoes, while others conveniently forgot and Jimmie cobbled their boots for nothing, at least for a time, until his sister saw them from her front window and sent in an account. But Jimmy mended many a shoe he knew he would never be paid for, and yet he hadn't the brazen heart to refuse, and there were those he repaired for a few coppers, knowing their owners were poor or had big families, and for the poorest of the poor, those who were on parish relief or the old-age pension (which was only ten-shillings a week) Jimmy sometimes forgot to tell his sister intentionally. And if she happened to see them in the shop he would only allow her to charge for the materials used; nothing for his work, sometimes charging only a few pence for long hours of work on the footwear of large starving families, rather than see the bairns go to school barefooted. Jimmie Duthie was the Good Samaritan who was never inside the kirk door; the anti-hypocrite who was more of a Christian than the elders whose boots he was obliged to lick. Jimmie hammered far into the night, when most of the village was asleep and the moon peering in at his window. In day time he could have been working in the country, his back to the village and its clutter of houses, before him the open parks and bird song, looking over the wide farmlands stretching up from the sea.

James Duthie's only real complaint with the world was that though his customers brought him plenty of work they seldom bought their footwear in his shop. Most of them went to Brochan, or even to Aberdeen, where they could buy them cheaper in the big stores, and have a holiday at the same time. Others dealt with mail order firms, especially the women folk and young quines, buying cheap trash that wore out in weeks; cardboard and wax they brought to Jimmie, and when he tried to sole them with real leather they fell to pieces, all for a few pence that wasn't worth the hours of sleep he lost over it.

Jimmie was a late riser and worked mostly at night, getting up at dinner time and hammering away till two or even three o'clock in the morning, his sister in bed, a light in his back window in the early hush of a summer morning, the first cocks crowing at Kingask, the seagulls winging inland from the sea, when Jimmie would retire at last, the mountain of work on the floor slightly reduced and grown into another heap, awaiting customers who didn't know their own boots, until the souter picked them out of the new miscellany, and even though you was a stranger he was seldom wrong in his identification.

But honest, hard working souter Duthie had a reason for

spreading his work load; for turning night into day. He liked working in the evenings when the back shop was full of farm workers and lads from the village, a gathering place for idle youth, after the Spittoon bar and the bus garage had closed, when all would flock to Jimmie Duthie's back shop for a news and a blether. Sometimes it was standing room only and the place so thick with fag reek you could hardly see Jimmie at his last by the darkened window, his tilley lamp hanging from a beam in the roof, sizzling away until somebody stood on a chair and pumped more air into it with the brass plunger and it brightened into life again. But Jimmie never stopped hammering, a string over the boot he was working at to hold it down on the last, looped over the instep of his left foot; his mouth full of sprigs, studs or tackets, taking them in his fingers one by one and plopping them into the new leather he had hammered on to somebody's worn-out shoes. Then he would take a seat by the coke stove, waxing thread with rosin and threading his needle, stitching a patch on the leatherwork of some bauchled old shoe, for he didn't have a machine and did all his sewing by hand.

Jimmie worked through all the banter between the farm chiels and the village lads, some of them fishermen, while others worked in Brochan; but he didn't like fighting and serious argument, and when this happened it was the only time he spoke up. But the teenagers respected Jimmie's quiet remonstrances and the quarrels never reached physical reaction; or if they did they went outside to settle their differences, but as the Castlebay constabulary was never far away they would shake hands peaceably in the cold darkness and sneak inside again to the warmth and comfort of the souter's coke stove in the back shop.

Constable Sim turned a blind eye and a deaf ear to the revelry in the souter's shop. There was no drink consumed on the premises, for Lizzie Duthie wouldn't allow it, and faith the bobby thought it kept the rascals off the street, where they might get up to worse mischief. So he thought he could go home after the pub closed to his wireless set by the fire, his big splay feet on a padded stool and his pipe alight, his tunic on the back of a chair, his peaked cap on a peg in the hall, with nothing to bother him unless the phone rang; which, thank heaven, wasn't often, and mostly his wife answered it, saying that the constable was still out on duty, unless it was a real urgent case, like somebody had set fire to the harbour or putten a sod on the minister's lum down at the Free Kirk manse, in which case he would have to get the firemen on the job, and they wouldn't thank him for that.

The story goes that when Constable Sim was a young bobby in the toon, and had charged a drunken youth for spitting on the pavement in Constitution Street, he fixed the lad by the lug and took him round the corner to spit in King Street, which was easier written down, because Sim couldn't spell Constitution Street, nor transcribe it from print to longhand though he had been looking at the nameplate on the wall. It was also rumoured of Sim about this time that he was summoned to the Police Inspector's office on a reprimand for being too lenient with young offenders. The Superintendent pointed out that this wasn't the way to get promotion; and at the same time insisting that every apprehension must be recorded, however trivial, even though it was only a drunk making his water up a close in the dark. So the next time that Constable Sim was out at night on his rounds, trying the locks on all the shop doors, he also flashed his torch up every lane, and when he came upon a young couple having intercourse against a back wall he flashed his torch right in the lad's face, blinding him for a moment and demanding: 'What's this ye're at min?' When the lad replied that surely the constable must know what he was at with a quine in his oxter Sim replied: 'Weel it's a damned good job ye wasna juist makin' yer watter or I'd a run ye in!' Folk said this was how he got his nickname – Pee-See Sim.

Another version of the story was that when Sim asked the youth what he was up to the lad said: 'Och nae naething constable!' Whereupon Sim handed him the torch and said: 'Stand aside than and maybe I'll mak' mair o't masell!' But knowing Sim as a respectable policeman a body is inclined to believe the earlier edition: the big clumsy brute that he was with his feet at ten-to-two on the clock, or one-fifty as a body would say nowadays; him that could hardly be bothered to throw his leg over a bicycle, never mind a woman.

The most ridiculous story about Pee-See Sim was the time that a sex starved sailor came off the train at dusk, determined to have the first prostitute he could find and take her up a dark pend for urgent intercourse. But there wasn't anything in skirts available for his purpose, nothing but a respectable middle-aged lady on crutches, so he grabbed hold of her with one hand and held the other on her mouth, then hustled her up the nearest pend, trailing her crutches behind her. He was doing his bit when Sim came into the close and tripped over the crutches in the gloamin': 'Shift yer barra oot o' that min,' he cries, searching for his torch – 'Ye're blockin' the traffic!' 'Aye, aye,' cries the lad, still gagging the woman, 'but hold on man till I ile the wheel!'

But Pee-See Sim had his good points too, and he didn't charge every lad he met in the mirk without a gas light on his bicycle. Like the cheil he met one dark night with two bicycles and only one light and that on the one he was riding, while he steered the other bike with his right hand, nearest the traffic, though there wasn't much of it in those days, only the odd car. Sim stepped out from the hedge and stopped the lad with his torch, grabbing the spare bike in passing, asking why there wasn't a light on this one. The lad replied that he only had one light and that he had only just bought the lady's cycle and he was taking it home to his sister, giving an address that the bobby knew. Sim asked the lad if he could take the spare bike on his left-hand side, away from the traffic, because he might cause an accident, but the cheil said that he couldn't hold it in his left hand and the bike would land in the ditch. 'Ah weel,' says Sim, 'tak' the licht aff yer land horse and put it on yer aff-side beast and we'll lat ye go wi' that!' Which shows that Constable Sim (for all his faults) had once been a farm-worker himself and knew about ploughing with horses and what he was talking about.

On another occasion Sim stopped a young farm servant on his motor-bike for speeding through the village. In the summer evenings he tore along the High Street like ricocheting thunder, endangering the lives of the bairns crossing the street, until the folk complained to Sim and he had to caution the lad. So the cheil stopped his machine in front of the bobby and left it ticking over until Sim had his particulars. Sim got out his notebook and licked his lead pencil and put his foot on the pillion, with his knee as a pad to write on. But the lad had heard about Sim and his spelling blunders and gave him an incredibly long and ridiculous name for the place he worked at, and while he spelled it out for the bobby and watched the puzzled look on his face he slipped his bike quietly into gear and sped off, leaving Sim standing in the High Street on one leg like a hen with cold feet in a farm close.

The last time Constable Sim was in Souter Duthie's shop at night – well he was hardly inside for the crowd of folk, but just had his head inside the door to show his authority, or that he was still around if anybody was looking for trouble; his long horse face white in the light of the tilley lamp, his hard topped cap at a bit of an angle on his balding head, and just touching the door lintel, for Sim was well over the six feet required to be a bobby. 'Inquisitive Sim' they called him because they said his curiosity would lead him up a gas pipe; or that he would speir the bloomers off a tinker's wife and then speir where she tint them. Anyway, Constable Sim was showing his silver buttons in the souter's shop when some ill-mannered devil let off a tremendous fart; a beer fart as you might call it, then looked at the bobby and called out: 'I bet ye couldna dae that Constable Sim withoot leavin' fern-tickles (freckles) on yer drawers!'

'Naw,' said the bobby, taking it in good humour: 'That's nae bad aff the dole!' Then he shut the door and disappeared, the souter's shop ringing with laughter.

Sometimes when a quine went into the shop the lads had their hands up her skirt, pulling the elastic of her knickers away from her bare hips and letting it back with a sharp snap. Some of the quines took it well enough but the next one would slap their faces. But of course the lads knew the ones to try it on with and they never molested strangers. Half-a-dozen quines of the village were regular visitors and sat on the counter of the back shop most of the evening, near Jimmie Duthie at his last, and being a bachelor he enjoyed the female comraderie; telling them jokes that made them skirl with laughter, kicking the counter with their wooden heeled shoes, their flimsy skirts well above their knees and the lads crowding round to hear the latest porn-kister.

Souter Duthie's was a great place for porn-kisters: the bars or dirty jokes the ploughmen told in their stables and chaumers or at the hoe, and if you wanted to hear the latest crack you just listened in the back shop at the souter's place.

There was the one about the two housemaids in the big house who were both invited to the same wedding; but their mistress wouldn't let them go, only one she said, as she didn't want to be

72

left alone. So the two lassies tossed a coin for the privilege of going to the wedding, their presents having been delivered beforehand, and they agreed that the one who won the toss should relate to the other all that went on at the wedding on her return, no matter how late it was. So one lass went to the wedding and the other stayed at home, sitting up in bed waiting for the news of the wedding. When the other quine returned and was taking off her clothes she was telling her friend the events of the evening: 'And you know,' she said, 'there was a man with a beard sitting at one side of the fireplace playing a big fiddle with its bottom on the floor and the stalk of it as high as his head, plucking the strings with one hand and scraping away with the bow in the other, and the big fiddle was saying "She's been bored afore! She's been bored afore!" Now on the other side of the fireplace there was a thin man with a bald head playing a little wee fiddle tucked up under his chin, sawing away at great speed with his bow, much quicker than the big fiddle, and it seemed to be saying "A-doot-it-A-doot-it, A-doot-it-A-doot-it!"'

After hearing that story, when the lads of the village saw a pregnant woman one would say 'The big fiddle's been there, nae the little ane!' and his companion would add 'A doot it, A doot it!'

Then there was the one about the country schoolmaster who became sexually involved with one of his girl pupils, and when he found himself in prison over it he asked his cell mate what he was in here for? 'Oh, for robbin' a waggon,' said the prisoner. 'Ah well,' said the dominie, 'I'm in here for waggin' ma robbin!'

And there was the dominie who couldn't sound his rs. Tipperary was a typical example and also his biggest stumbling block, so he told his scholars: 'Don't you say Tippawayway as I say Tippawayway – just you say Tippawayway wight away!'

Jimmie Duthie liked the stories, conundrums, riddles and tongue-twisters, no matter how often he heard them, and new versions of the same story were always welcome. Sometimes he repeated one himself, one he had heard from a customer or a traveller during the day, and one of his favourites was about the woman who had left the village a long time back and had returned to look up her old friend and neighbour Mrs Bile. But in her absence Mrs Bile had left the village and nowhere could she find her. The woman tried everywhere but nobody could tell her where Mrs Bile had moved to. She tried the Post Office, the Police, the Fire Station, even the doctor and the banker and most of the shops, but she was none the wiser. On leaving the village the woman met the postman on his bicycle and she thought now this was the man who should know the whereabouts of Mrs Bile. So she hailed the postie and when he got off his bike she cried out: 'I say postie, excuse me, but have ye got a bile on yer roote?' 'Oh fie na woman,' says the postie, somewhat taken aback, 'but I've got a blin' lump on my backside ridin' this bicycle!'

The next time you was down at Jimmie Duthie's with your tackety boots for repair; heels, toes and tackets as they said, he told you about the loon who had been in the other day with his father's boots for cobbling, and he told the souter to keep the right toe well back, and when Jimmie asked why he should do that the loon replied 'because that's the one he kicks my arse with!'

Then Jimmie asked you how the Queen Mary was doing and where you kept it, and when you said upstairs he said nobody would see it there; such a pity to keep a thing like that out of sight, like keeping your candle under a bushel, why not bring it down and he would display it in his front window? Oh, he would watch the bairns that they didn't tamper with it, though it wasn't likely they would go behind the counter. He would get his sister to tidy up the window and remove the odd pair of shoes; such a grand place for your boat, where everybody in the village could see it, and anybody passing through, maybe even someone who would buy it, and then you could have a sideline making boats.

So you brought the Queen Mary down from Kingask on your bicycle, the giant model stanced on the saddle and handlebars, while you pushed the bike along very carefully, the village loons chasing after you to see the boat and to watch where you was going with it. Lizzie Duthie had cleared the unsold shoes from the front window for the ship and you placed it there while the bairns gathered outside for a grandstand view.

The Queen Mary aroused considerable interest in the village, especially among the fisher folk, and a great many people admired

74

your handiwork, going inside to ask Jimmie about the ship and who had made it; even some of the farmers of the parish, who, unlike the blacksmith, thought it was a fine piece of craftsmanship. But nobody seemed keen on buying it or even asking about the price. Maybe the size was against it, because it nearly filled the souter's window and it would be expensive making a glass case for that size of a ship. The only real reaction was that when Trail the grocer's son saw the ship he wanted you to make a model for him, though much smaller, a steam drifter, which you did; entirely from cardboard this time, without the leather hull, as he didn't want it for sailing, only for show, and he had the joiner make a glass case for it and kept it in his bedroom. Constable Sim had a look at the liner, and bent down to examine it more closely, his peaked cap under his arm and putting on his glasses, but he made no offer of purchase.

Lizzie Duthie cleaned up the front shop for the occasion, dusted the shelves and tidied up the boxes of unsold shoes, polished the window, shook out the mats and swept the floor. But Lizzie couldn't tackle the back shop, so all the youths who gathered in the evenings put their heads together and cleared out the souter's back shop, and Lizzie covered your boat with brown paper before they started because of the dust. Five barrow loads of solid rubbish they carted out and buried it deep down in the kailyard at the back; swept the place clean with byre brooms and Lizzie's rug brush for the corners; arranged the mountains of shoes on separate shelves and Lizzie gave them all their tea for their trouble. Now you could stand in the middle of the floor and there was room for chairs, and Jimmie's only complaint was that he couldn't find his tools; his awl and his beetle, turcas and chisel, after the spring-clean. Things were where they should be but the souter was happier in a muddle; or what seemed a muddle to ither folk, though Jimmie knew instinctively where everything was in his own eccentric way. He was even finding it difficult to trace the shoes of his customers on the shelves, something that had never bothered him while they were in a heap on the floor.

But Jimmie Duthie never recovered from that dust up, and though the lads meant well they were merely tidying up the place for his funeral. He had coughed through it all and had hoasted for days after it, until he had a lung haemorrhage and was taken away to hospital, where the doctors discovered from x-rays that Jimmie Duthie had lung cancer. He had been a dying man for years though nobody ever knew it, and if he suspected it himself he never complained. His sister was the delicate one and never far from death's door; frail and sallow faced, like the leather her brother worked with, her body wracked with only forty years of living, yet she survived Jimmie for many lonely years and lived in the same house till the end of her days.

Jimmie had a fag hoast for years but the spring-clean brought his illness to a crisis. In the months that followed his condition degenerated. Mostly in those days it was called decline or tuberculosis, the patient just wasting away and nothing anybody could do to revive him; a condition which, unfortunately, has not improved in modern times, though a little more can be done to ease the suffering, like pain killers and taking fluid from the lungs.

Though Jimmie was sent home from hospital his shop was never the same again. His customers dwindled and took their work to Tackie Broon, while folk stared at your boat in Jimmie's window in the clean empty shop and the wasted figure bending over the last. When Jimmie wasn't to be seen they sometimes rapped on the house door to ask for the souter, but Lizzie shook her tousled head and said he was still in bed and wouldn't be able to work that day. He had given up his beloved indoor bowling and shuttlecock and now his shop was closed almost every day.

The last time you saw Jimmie was in the back shop, a pale unshaven creature with the look of death in his sunken eyes; the shrivelled skin stretched over the bones of his face, while he leaned painfully on the counter for support, though strangely enough the cough no longer bothered him, maybe because he had given up smoking. You asked permission to take away your boat and Jimmie said he was sorry he hadn't been able to sell it for you; always thinking of other people before himself as usual. A few weeks after this Jimmie had a lung collapse and died in hospital, and his funeral was one of the largest ever seen in the village. After his death his sister put a notice in the paper claiming all debts owing to her late brother; but all you owed Jimmie Duthie was gratitude and respect for one of the most generous hearted of men you had ever known in your life, a martyr almost of his own selflessness.

But now you had to go to Tackie Broon with the others for your shoe repairs, and on your very first visit he asked about that boat of yours that was in Jimmie Duthie's window before he died. Did he want to buy it you asked. No, he said, he wouldn't offer you money for it; such things were beyond monetary value – 'but take a look round the shop: see all these fine birds in their cages? . . . Well, you can pick any bird you fancy, cage and all, and you can have it for your boat!'

So you swopped the Queen Mary for a budgerigar in a hanging cage, something that would be easier flitted at the Term than a giant boat. And Tackie Broon would have a glass case made for your ship he said where it wouldn't gather dust, for already you had been trying to clean it with a bellows and sweeping the decks with a feather.

Jockie the green and yellow budgie lived for two years in his gilded cage and became the darling pet of little Brian; though by this time he had grown out of the adjective and stood as high as your waist. But Jockie developed the same symptoms as Jimmie Duthie and pined away in his cage, drooping his green feathers and blinking his eyes for want of proper bird seed during the war. Brian cried his eyes out when Jockie died and wouldn't give him up for burial, hiding him under the cushion of an armchair, believing he would revive with the heat of the fire. He even had his mother fill a hot water bottle, blaming her for starving Jockie to death, which of course was a false statement. Eventually he buried Jockie at the foot of the garden, and with a tearful face he set a small cross of fir on the tiny grave and a saucer filled with water.

But in the years that followed you sometimes wondered just how much longer Jimmie Duthie would have lived if the Queen Mary had never been built.

Mutch of the Puddockstyle!

Faith but he was a strushle brute Bert Mutch, never even dressed himsel' for the marts or a roup, juist oot o' the byre in his sharny boots and away on his bike wi' a piece in his pooch, an unlit fag between his thick sulky lips (and most likely it would still be hangin' there when he came back in the afternoon) for he was loth to light a fag when it lasted longer chewing it, and saved bawbees forbye, juist as a piece in his pooch saved him buying his dinner, and the bicycle saved his bus fare, for in Jehova's life nothing was so important as money.

The folks round about called him Jehova because he never swore, always respected the Lord's name and used 'By Jove!' instead, his biggest swear word though the roan mare had stood on his foot with an iron heel, or he had chapped his thoom with a claw-hammer; though it sounded more like 'By Chove!' to the farming folk, so they didn't know what to make of it and just called him 'Jehova!' It wasn't out of any ill-will they called him names, but just for the fun of the thing, never thinking they were sinners taking the Lord's name in vain. Not that he was a kirk-going body, for the cheil could never be bothered to rig himself for a pulpit meeting, though he never drank or chased the quines either.

But the folk had never quite forgiven the cheil since he kicked his fee-ed loon doon the chaumer stair for sleepin'-in; tore him out of bed in his sark tail and kicked him on the bare doup with his tackety boot, nearly breaking the lad's neck in the fall. 'By Chove!' he cried, from the top of the stair, 'that'll learn ye tae rise in the mornin', and ye'll get no breakfast for yer pains. Get yer breeks on and yoke yer horse or ye'll get mair!' He went hammerin' down the timmer steps and loupit over the crumpled heap at the bottom, off to the byre in his ill-temper, thinking maybe that would be the end of it, the halflin being an orphan and nobody to speak up for him.

78

The lad got warsled up the stair, bruised and swelling, and sat on the bed a while, greeting, nearly a grown man but feared to lift his hand to Jehova. He put on his claes and hirpled over the grass parks to the cottar wife at Shinbrae that did his washing, the only hame he knew since he came out of the orphanage in Glasgow yonder. The woman had loons of her ain on the fairms, and when she saw the cheil come hytering over the close and had looked at his sores and heard his story she was fair roused and sent him straight to the bobby, and she said that the loon could bide with her or he got anither place. The Sheriff's Officer and a bobby came out from Brochan and had a look at the chaumer at the Puddockstyle, a bit loft over the stable with nothing in it but a box-bed and a chair, not a spark of fire and a bit skylight on the slated roof. The seams were stuffed with old newspapers to keep out the draught and there was a rat hole in the wall skirting and mice dirt on the floor. They had a look at the steep stair where the loon had bruised his hurdies, and no wonder they thought when they saw the depth of it. They cornered Mutch in the byre and he was fair taken aback and they told him that anything he might say would be taken down in evidence against him, and all that palaver, and then they said he was to be charged with malicious behaviour and assault with injury and for taking the law into his own hands. The Procurator Fiscal gave him a further reprimand in the court-house for his ill-treatment of his servant and said that the accused was fortunate that the youth hadn't suffered worse injury, and that orphans had to be protected from tyrants like himself in industry. A lawyer cheil stuck up for Mutch and said that the youth was loose-living and stayed up late at night and spent all his money on smoking and drink and girls, pestering the accused for 'subs' or advance payments of his wages almost every week from a six-months' contract, besides over-sleeping in the mornings. But the loon had a solicitor as well and he conceded that the accused had paid the youth weekly from his six-months' wages contract, due at the Term, but he said there was no evidence that the young man was a profligate, and even if he had been he should have been given a warning on his behaviour, and a chance to mend his ways, instead of which he had been brutally assaulted by the accused. The Fiscal fined Mutch £10 and warned him on his future conduct, ordering that he pay the defendant the balance of his wages yet owing to him, and to stamp his Insurance card to date as the lad wouldn't be returning to his employment; and furthermore the accused must put a fireplace in his bothy or build a new one for the accommodation of future employees. It was all a bit of a stamagaster for Mutch of the Puddockstyle and it made him think twice before he lifted his hand again (or his foot) to a working body about his place.

Mutch had been a long time single, near forty when his mither died and never a woman in his life. As an old creature, frail and sair from the chauve of the Puddockstyle, the widow sometimes wondered what would become of the cheil when she was under the green sod, for she had trauchled on her lane without a serving quine to tempt him from his bachelor ways. But at the end of her tether the old woman wasna able and she was forced to fee a kitchie quine, an ill-faured creature with a hare-lip stammer and a squint eye that couldn't get a place easily and wasn't likely to arouse any strange feelings in her son. Now that his mither had gone the quine washed his fule sark and sewed a button on his breeks and cooked a bit meat; she was cheap and strong and could melk the kye and ca' the churn and mak' butter and cheese and siller and pleased the man fine though he didna share her bed.

Back in the old days you would have seen Mrs Mutch weeding carrots in the windswept parks, down on her knees with an old waterproof on her shoulders and a scarf about her head; a sturdy big-boned woman that could handle a fork like a man and was never afraid of the glaur or the chauve of the farm wife. In her young day she had hoed in her bare feet, with her pram on the end-rig, all these years ago till her bairn got bigger and began to take an interest in the place. Her man had died young of a bowel complaint, struggling to the end the breet, pulling turnips on his knees when he should have been under the blankets, even on a Sunday, and kirk-going folk thought he was beyond redemption, but never gave the man any help to feed his nowt beasts; not that he cared, for he had an independent turn of mind and a game wife that could take her turn at the wark with the best of them. But that was a long time back, and when her man died the mistress of the Puddockstyle put most of her place to grass and leased the parks for grazing, working the rest of it with her loon when he came of age; maybe spoiling him a bit in his youth, for want of a man, so that he soon began to show her that he was the boss.

While Bert Mutch was still at the school some of the neighbours ploughed the widow's fields and gave her some help with the hairst, until one of them tried to take advantage of her in the barn, when young Mutch came over his back with a horse yoke and sent the scoundrel hirpling home to his wife with a different story to tell. From then on the widow and her son managed on their own and the loon was between the plough stilts while he was still at the school. In his teens he ploughed in all the parks for cropping again and fee-ed a single man for the chaumer, giving him the pair of horses to work while he sorted the nowt himsel', with a bit of dealing at the marts and roups on the side.

But over the years young Mutch had never changed, and in his middle-age he still went about like a tink and chewed his fags to make them last; still cycled to mart or roup to save his bus fare, and still carried a piece in his pooch to save the expense of buying his dinner. Some of his neighbours had got the length of a motor car and had sold their gigs and shelts and went tearing past Mutch on his bicycle on his way to the mart, sometimes nearly running him down by the way he swaggered about on the road, his thoughts deep in nowt and corn and siller, his sharny boots on the pedals and his long coat getting in the spokes of his back wheel, nearly throwing him off balance on a windy day; a rain squall slashing at his red face, his wet fag drooping from his stubbly mouth, his bonnet tilted to one side on his grey, balding head.

Some of the neighbours had offered Mutch a lift once or twice, trying to show off their new cars, sneering in his face when he refused, and saying among themselves that he would be safer on the bus, but that most likely he grudged the fare. They were inclined to look down their noses at Mutch, though they knew he was better off than they were: Them with their thriftless wives and big families and new cars, and him still a single man running a bicycle and his pound notes stuffed into moggans and stockings and a big band-box under his bed, under lock and key, 'cause he wouldn't trust a banker with it or pay tax if he could help it. Hadn't the hare-lip quine seen him at the band-box when she was polishing the stairs, surrounded by stacks of coin and paper wads, like a miser over his gold? And the ill-gotten creature had lisped out her excited story to the grocer's vanman at the gable of the kitchie; the one who always lifted her frock or took a pinch at her bare hip when he closed the van door, the quine laughing and slivering down her chin, not to mention what he might have tried with her behind a whin bush, or anywhere else that was handy, had he not been fear't that Mutch or his man would be watching from some glory hole about the Puddockstyle.

But in spite of his greed for wark and siller Mutch had a still greater hankering for a wife and bairns to share it. For all his rough ways he was at heart deeply human. His meanness he couldn't help and going about like a tramp never harmed anyone. He got great satisfaction in scrimping himself, in saving bawbees where others were spending. But as the years grew upon him, and especially since his mither died, Mutch felt a great need for a family to share it; for an heir to take over what he had gathered and scraped to save, for without this the man felt a great emptiness in his drizzen life; a hollow knocking from within, for he was not the true miser and his grasping seemed without purpose. But getting the right wife was chancey, aye faith! He would have to ca' canny aboot that.

Now you would have thought that if the cheil was looking for a wife he would have spruced himself up a bit; but na na, still went about ill-clad and hungry looking, like he didn't have a copper to spare; but maybe he thought that if it was dress and gear that the woman was after she wasn't for him, aye faith it was chancey. But he would bide his time or he found the right woman to share his bed and look after his bawbees. He knew fine there were randies in the Bogside who envied his money hoard and a chance to share in it, but he never gave them a chance to untie his bootlaces, or to put him to bed in a drunken stupor, for he never attended any of their jamborees, concerts or dances; nothing where the limmers could get their grasping fingers into his pockets, neither at the pictures or the fairs, so that by the time he was forty the spinsters in the Bogside had given up trying to invite Mutch to any of their goings on and left him to his bachelor wiles with the hare-lip and his treasure kist.

But at mart or roup he could out-bid his neighbours for anything that he wanted, like a good thriving steer or a gelding that took his fancy; especially if he thought that by selling again he could make a pound or two, which he usually did, for he could see that if anyone wanted something badly enough to bid with him to the last shilling they wouldn't grudge a little more to have it at the second chance. He was a sharp dealer at the ringsides and sometimes made a damned sight more than he ever did on the fairm, with all its pleiter. Some folk hinted that he should make a full time job of it, and put the fairm back in grass; a collar and tie job, which was maybe a jibe at his greasy sark, but Mutch said it was risky and that he'd keep it as a side line. But with a wink or a nod to the auctioneer he could sometimes take money out of thin air, chewing on his fag and eyeing up the beasts and gear with a wizard's instinct for a bargain.

But the more money he made the shabbier he grew, and a wife seemed as far away as ever. Mony a neighbour's wife said she would enjoy giving him a good scrub and a new rig-out of clothes, for he was a man well built and with fairly good looks, though as things were folk began to steer clear of him for the smell of his unwashed body. It was a wonder, they thought, that the hare-lip didn't look after him better, even though she didn't share his bed, for she might share his will, seeing that the cheil had nobody else to leave it to directly, unless it were some distant cousins who never looked near him, though they might attend his funeral, should anything happen to the stock, to see if there was anything left for them at the bone picking.

But for all their claik the cheil bided his time, and by and bye, at the roup on Whirliebrae he met a woman body that took his fancy. Above all the steer of the folk and the scrachin' of hens and the howling of nowt he noticed the woman as soon as he came off his bike and took the clips out of his breeks. The fine head of her, upstanding as a high priced ornament, the brown gold of her hair, plaited and spun into a bun on the nape of her neck, the wide-brimmed hat shading her pleasant features, soft appealing eyes with a sparkle in her glances, her small nose slightly tilted at the tip, and her rather wide mouth always on the brink of a smile; the gold pendant on her bare, open breast, the frilled pink blouse, velvet tunic and a half-pleat tartan skirt, narrow at the waist and flared out wide just under her knees, silk stockings on her shapely calfs and buckles on her little black shoes; and the jaunty spring of her walk as she picked her way over the grass and the dubs of the farm close, swinging her soft skirt in a grace of movement that fair caught a body's eye.

Mutch had no eye for the nowt that sunny day of early May, or for the sturdy geldings that were trotted out for the farmers around the close. He was bewitched by the woman and couldn't take his gaze away from her. The auctioneer looked in vain for his customary wink while he whacked the wooden pailing with his stick. Mutch shunned his searching eyes that were darting over the crowd, stick raised in the air, poised, waiting, lingering, then down with a smack to the last bidder. But Mutch wasn't interested; his thoughts that day were all of the woman. Where had she gone? He must watch and follow her.

For the first time in his life he realized that this was something money couldn't buy; something he eagerly wanted but the last bid would count for nothing. She wasn't for sale. For the first time also he suddenly became aware of himself; of the tramp he was among all the folk that were dressed, and he took the fag from his mouth and threw it in the myre. He had a mind to fly home and rig himself like for a funeral, the only decent suit he had; but there was no time, the woman might be off or he got back. She would have to be put to the test, rags and all, and By Jove she was worth it! His only chance was to watch what the woman bought, or tried to buy, and he must out-bid her for it, price was no obstacle; then maybe he could tempt her with a second chance. The idea came to him in a flash; one of his old tricks with a new and definite purpose, the only way he could buy the unsaleable.

The cattle sale was over and the auctioneer was striding over the park to the rows of implements, all painted and numbered, the clerk at his heels with pencil and notebook and a troop of folk crowding round. But there was no sign of the woman in the flared tartan skirt. Ah well it must be the furniture sale she was after and Mutch strode round to the close, to the farmhouse, where some few were gathered, mostly women, coming and going from the kitchen, where they were permitted to look at the articles for sale. He was about to go inside when the woman came to the door, her violet eyes looking him in the face, but with no disdain in them, no resentment of his ragged appearance; kind they were

84

and smiling as she stepped aside to let him pass. Now he must wait and watch; he mustn't let her out of his sight again while the sale lasted.

It was a long time to Mutch but at last the auctioneer came round with the folk and the sale began around the kitchen door. Mutch kept his head down, his gaze away from the auctioneer; watching the woman, her every move, every gesture, every look, but so far she made no bid. The auctioneer stuck with a sale and cried out his name in a joke, for Mutch usually saw him out, but today he took no notice; he didn't want to become involved. He was watching the woman.

Several things had gone: tables, chairs, pictures, carpets, rugs, and now a suite, and still no bid from the woman. Then someone brought ben a wag-at-the-wa' clock, polished wood with bold figures and coloured pictures on its face, brass chains and weights slung underneath; a solid thing, so that the bearer could hardly hold it up for the ring of folk round the door to see it. The auctioneer began with his usual patter, pointing at the clock with his stick. '. . . How much am I bid then? Who'll say fifty pounds, forty, thirty, twenty, ten, a fiver? . . . who will give me a start then? . . . One pound, ten bob, five bob? . . . Thanks lady, five bob I'm bid; five, ten, fifteen, a pound,' his stick flicking over the crowd and always coming back to the lady at the door. So that was what she was on! But he would bide his time; no need to make it dearer than was necessary, and the bidding was brisk yet. He would catch her on the last hop, when the others had been weeded out – when she thought the prize was hers. His eyes and ears were needle sharp. 'Fourteen pounds,' the auctioneer was saying, resorting to one-pound bids. 'Come on, the brass chains are worth more than that – fifteen pounds, sixteen, seventeen, eighteen . . .' But the bids were slowing down, slower yet. Mutch stood on his toes to watch the crowd. Four or five hands still going up, now four, now three. 'Twenty-seven pounds, twenty-eight . . .' It was risky. What if the woman should fall out? Ah well, he would buy the clock in any case. What, another bidder? Somebody must be nodding; or maybe just a wink. Surely he wouldn't be taking bids out of the air for a clock at that price? 'Thirty-one pounds . . . thirty-two . . .' The lady was still there and the stick came back to her, level with her daintily tilted nostril.

She hesitated, shook her head slowly . . . 'I'll take ten bob,' the auctioneer was saying, and she went on, on. 'Thirty-five, thirty-five-and-a-half . . .' Mutch could wait no longer and he whistled the auctioneer, the lady far too concerned even to notice it. The stick was pointed straight in his face. 'Thirty-five-pounds-ten sir,' the auctioneer treating him like a stranger but fully in his confidence; aware of his move to boost the bidding, whatever the purpose. 'Thirty-six . . . thirty-six-and-a-half . . .' Now it was Mutch and the woman, ding dong, ding dong, but he won, and he took the clock in his great oxter and went away over by the stable door to set the thing down safely somewhere.

He went over to the open window at the farmhouse and handed in his payment to the cashier, who gave him a receipt, and when he went back to the clock the woman was looking at it, just what he expected her to do. 'I did so want it,' she said quietly, disappointment clearly in her face. 'But you out-bid me for it. I couldn't afford all that money anyway. I don't know what came over me!'

'Folks lose their heads at roups,' Mutch remarked, 'and they throw money aboot like cauld watter.'

Her soft velvet eyes creamed over his face and he thought that little more would bring them to tears.

'Would ye still be wanting the clock then, Miss . . .'

'Oh yes . . . Joyce Allardyce is the name. I'm from the manse at Bourie,' and she held out her white gloved hand.

'Mutch is my name, Miss Allardyce; Bert Mutch frae the fairm o' Puddockstyle yonder, in the Bogside.'

They shook hands, her gloved fingers warm and tender in his big rough fist.

'Oh yes, Mr Mutch, I still want the clock. In fact I came here on a special errand to get it. But it's out of the question now. I just couldn't afford all that money.'

'What would ye be willin' to pay for it than?'

'So you would sell it again, Mr Mutch?'

'That was the general idea. Name yer price! The most you could afford to pay for it.'

'Oh but I couldn't. It's beyond my reach; you paid thirty-nine pounds for it, an awful lot of money for a clock. My brother would be so upset.'

'Your brither, Miss Allardyce?'

'Yes, you see, he's the minister at Bourie and I've been his housekeeper since his wife died two years ago.'

'Oh I see,' and Mutch was overwhelmed with a sudden burst of generosity.

'Well I'll let you have the clock for twenty-five pounds,' he said. 'Could you manage that?'

'Oh but you couldn't Mr Mutch; it's a shame, and you'd be selling at a loss.'

'I dinna usually deal in clocks, Miss Allardyce, so let's say that I was a bit rash in buying it.'

'And you are determined to let me have it for twenty-five pounds?'

'Aye, and it's a grand clock, I think!'

'It is, lovely. But you must have a reason for this, Mr Mutch.'

'Well I would be glad to get it off my hands, and I was a bit sorry to see you disappointed; the sad look on yer face when ye looked at the clock after the sale. You was nearly greetin' lass, and ye look sae much bonnier smilin'.'

A faint blush heightened the colour on her cheeks. 'Thank you Mr Mutch. But it's so sweet of you; and if I take the clock how can I repay you?'

'Never mind that. Where will we put the clock? Have we time for a wee cup of tea to seal the bargain?'

'Oh that would be nice! I have my car Mr Mutch. Oh yes I'll take the clock, though it makes me feel ashamed Mr Mutch, and I don't know what my brother will say. He has his scruples you see, being a minister. Perhaps if you would carry the clock over to the car for me.' And she fumbled in her small handbag for the money.

Mutch carried the clock over to the car and she gave him the twenty-five pounds, mostly in fivers, though he never counted it but thrust it into his hip pocket. 'You could always say the devil tempted you Miss Allardyce,' he said, with a sulky laugh, 'or just never let on. Say you paid twenty-five pounds for the clock and keep it a secret between us.'

'Oh but I couldn't deceive him, Mr Mutch; not for the world, and some of the congregation might tell him what the clock was sold at. I even spotted one or two of our Elders in the crowd.

You'll just have to come up to the manse sometime Mr Mutch and explain it.'

'Ah well Miss Allardyce, I'll be quite willin' tae do that, though I am a bit bashful meetin' gentry folk.'

Miss Allardyce smiled at his awkwardness and the way he put it. 'Oh but we will make you feel quite at home Mr Mutch; have no fear about that.'

It was getting chilly and she took her coat out of the car and put it on, Mutch holding it out for her. They went to the marquee in the grass park, where there was a smell of cigarette smoke and brewing tea, the clatter of dishes, voices and laughter. They found a small table for two near a tent pole and Mutch ordered tea and cakes for two, holding up his hand when Miss Allardyce tried to forestall him.

They waited shyly, facing each other, and both looked around the tent.

'I hope you won't mind, Miss Allardyce, me being such a track, like; but I juist came oot of the coo byre,' falling through his English.

'Of course not, Mr Mutch. I know how it is with farming people. And you can call me Joyce if you like.'

'Thank ye, Miss Allardyce; I mean Miss Joyce. Folk usually call me Bert, but I'd prefer Bertie, if you don't mind.' He thought better not to tell her his nickname. It wasn't funny.

He felt an awful gowk in her genteel presence, among all the toffs that were dressed and respectable, and him like a tink in his shabby waterproof, the tails of it on the grass, his piece still in his pocket; his baggy trousers glazed with dirt, his boots as grey as the road.

A waitress came and spread out the tea things in front of them from a tray.

So they had a fair crack over the tea leaves, the two of them, the lady and the tramp as you might say, each trying to find out as much as possible about the other, in a round about sort of way; two shy people who had never seen much of the other's side of life.

'I'm an aul' tea-wife masel',' Mutch assured her, pouring a second cup for both of them, and Miss Allardyce smiled to hear it.

But she fair opened up the heart of the cheil, and the honeyed smile softened his hard exterior; winning him over in a way he would never have believed possible with the women folk. It was a new experience to the clumsy cheil and he blethered the gist of his life story with his big mouth full of apple-tart. Miss Allardyce sipped her tea, listened and smiled under her wide-brimmed hat, her brown gold hair against her lillied cheeks, two small pearls at her ear-lobes that the cheil hadn't noticed before. But the violet depths of those wondrous eyes changed the colour of his skies; swept away all clouds, and the sun was shining on autumn woods and golden harvest fields, green parks where kine were fed on milk and honey, and the sweet fragrance of her perfume filled the land with her presence.

The cheil was so much taken out of himself that before he realized what he was saying he blurted out that he would pay for both teas. He could hardly believe his ain lugs when he heard himself speaking, and surely he would have to take himself to task about it when it was all over. Him that had never given a penny to a bairn or a crust of bread to a tinker wife, and here he was treating this genteel stranger to a High Tea which, in normal circumstances, he would have grudged even for himself, gloating over the cost that his self-denial had spared him.

But he wasn't himself that day the cheil and he paid gladly for both teas, softly rebuking the woman when she offered him money, and he considered it a bargain for the riches that their meeting had brought him.

He walked her back to the car park, past the beer tent, where the drunks were leering at the door flap, throwing taunts at his back, one calling out: 'Aye Jehova!' But he took no notice, and neither apparently did Miss Allardyce. The sale was almost over and folk would soon be taking the road, though the sun was still well up in the sky.

Miss Allardyce was seated at the wheel of her little Morris car, the precious clock in the back seat. She pulled the starter and the car purred smoothly. Mutch was standing by the door, the handle in his grip, loth to let the woman go; watching those diamonds that sparkled in her eyes while her parting smile caressed his weary heart. He would take the old cart road from Whirliebrae, a grass-grown short-cut to the Puddockstyle, in the other direction from Miss Allardyce.

'Maybe at some other sale I'll see you again Miss Joyce, and next time I'll be better dressed.'

'Oh never mind that Mr Mutch – or should I call you Bertie? You have been so good to me; and if you are not too bashful we shall be delighted to welcome you sometime at the manse of Bourie.'

'Oh that would be grand Miss Joyce. I sall certainly look forrard to seeing you again. I'll close your door than and be off. Ta-ta Miss Joyce. I hope we'll meet again!'

The car moved off down the grass brae and the cheil lifted his hand in a wave of farewell, rather sadly, with a nip in his eyes that made them moist. He sighed at her going, the lovely Miss Allardyce, while he went to get his bicycle.

Bert Mutch could safely say it had been one of the happiest days of his bachelor life when he met Miss Allardyce, for he certainly believed he had fallen in love with the creature; and maybe she with him he hoped, by the way she spoke, so friendly like. From what he had gathered she would be in her thirties: a spinster body who kept house for her brother, who was the minister at Bourie, not that he knew the place very well, only in passing, but in his present mood it wouldn't be long or he was visiting in that direction.

It was a wonder he thought that a good looking woman like that was still single, but maybe that was something he should be thankful for and nae ask questions that were none o' his business. And efter a', her brither had tae hae somebody for a hoose-keeper, seein' his poor wife had died. And maybe Miss Allardyce would have a pucklie siller behind her, bein' come o' the clergy like, so she wouldn't come empty handed to the Puddockstyle, and she looked like a body that could be trusted with what he had already. Maybe it was a pity that she wasna of the farming stock, and could melk a coo or churn butter, though her hands were too lady like for that, white as lilies and the scent of her as sweet. There wasn't the likes of her in the Bogside or he'd have been married long ago. Ah weel but he could mak' her a lady and the hare-lip would do the wark; aye, that was a better idea, and that would gie the neighbour folk something tae craw aboot – a lady at the Puddockstyle. What's mair, maybe he could buy a motor car and start a new life athegither, aye faith!

90

It was at this point he suddenly realized he was on his bicycle, spinning down the brae from the roup. He had no recollection of leaving the sale, so engrossed was he in his future plans to be almost in a trance, carried away with his thoughts of Miss Allardyce and the manse of Bourie.

He had never been a kirk body but By Chove he never swore and it wasn't likely he'd say an ill werd in front of Miss Allardyce. Oh aye, he'd had to pay for his sanctimony, for there were ill-mannered folk who took the size of him, and made a joke of his swear words, and had given him a nickname, the blasphemous heathens, for he had overheard them from time to time calling him Jehova! But they'd pay for it yet, those sons of Satan, for the good Lord would protect his ain, and once he had Miss Allardyce under his care he would surely be doubly blessed.

And surely he would have a family too. Oh aye, a loon for a start to take over the Puddockstyle, and maybe a dother or twa later on, Miss Allardyce wasn't too old for that yet. All things in their time; everything comes to him who waits he had heard it said, and he had waited well and lang for this great day.

He was speeding down the long brae but hardly aware of it, his thoughts on wings of romance, never heeding the dead-end cross-roads at the foot of the hill, where the track from Whirliebrae joined the main road, and the odd motor car that was passing there. He never dachled but sped on deep in thought, gnawing on his drooping fag, his waterproof flapping behind him, the whin and broom obscuring his view of the main road, where everybody had the right of way, and at the last moment he applied the brakes on his bicycle.

But alas too late, for he was on the main road before he noticed, smack in front of a car at slashing speed. There was a screech of brakes and a scream of tyre skids and Mutch was tossed into the air over the bonnet of the car and catapulted head first against the stone dyke, his body hitting the wall with such force he rebounded back on to the road.

The car climbed the bank avoiding him but bounced back on to the road when it stopped, some twenty yards from the crossing. Two farming like cheils came out of it, staggering a bit, as they hurried back to the bleeding man on the road. They stood over him, wondering if he was dead. One of them bent down unsteadily

91

and turned him over so that he could see his face. 'God almighty,' he cried, 'it's Bert Mutch!' The other man hiccoughed. 'Who the hell's Bert Mutch?' he asked. His companion swayed a little as he stood up, spreading out his hands, his fingers tipped with blood. 'Why,' he cried, 'the bastard that threw me doon the chaumer stair at Puddockstyle!'

Blood was seeping from Mutch's ears and mouth and a small pool was gathering on the road. His cap had gone and there was an ugly gash on his head.

'Is he dead then?' the other asked.

The younger man kneeled down again, feeling awkwardly for Mutch's pulse and listening for his breathing. 'I'm nae sure,' he replied, 'but I think he's still breathin'.'

'Ripe his pooches,' the older man ordered, lighting a fag.

The youth on the road went through Mutch's pockets, starting with his coat. 'Just a piece,' he shouted, throwing out the jam sandwiches. Then he tried the jacket. 'Ah, a pocket-book or wallet or something; now I'll try the hip pooch. Ah, something here, a bundle of notes, aye, OK.'

The other man was getting impatient, watching the road. 'Come on,' he cried, tugging at his companion, 'let's get tae hell oot o' here; we dinna want onybody tae catch us here, smellin' like a distillery, especially the cops. Come on Mike, for Christ's sake!'

He ran forward to the car and tore the mangled bicycle from under the front axle and threw it against the dyke.

'But I didna mean tae kill him,' the other protested, now stricken with sudden remorse, the blood speckled notes in his hands. 'God knows, he didna give me a chance tae spare him!' He stood half-way between the car and his old employer lying on the road. Tears now glistened his eyes and he threw the money in the air. 'I dinna want it,' he cried, 'I didna mean tae kill him!'

His companion came running back and gathered up the wallet and the scattered bank notes, bundled the weeping youth into the passenger seat and slammed the car door. 'I'll drive,' he yelled and threw away his cigarette, then ran round the car to the driver's side. Even as he drove off another car was in his mirror, but he soon lost it when it stopped beside the body. After all it wasn't really their fault that Mutch's thoughts were so far away that late afternoon, and not on the road he travelled, but with Miss Joyce Allardyce at the manse of Bourie.

Cap in the Wind

It was towards the end of your first summer at Kingask that you had a visit from your old school pal Bryce Holt, who had been Best Man at your wedding; him that had been so taken with your pretty Kathleen before you married her, though he never had a chance to go courting with her, but made it plain enough in his looks and with an occasional remark on how much he admired your choice of a bride. You had been milk boys together in your schooldays, selling milk in the toon from his father's milk cart, and though he was a farmer's son and you was only a cottar loon he had always treated you as an equal; sharing his tips and his chocolate on Saturday mornings when the housewives paid their milk. But in the two years since your marriage you had forgotten all about Bryce and his infatuation for Kathleen, and as you hadn't seen him since your wedding day you thought he had forgotten about it too. But apparently he hadn't, nor had he gotten a lass of his own, or if he had she had jilted him, though God knows why, for Bryce was a handsome cheil and a farmer's son and you would have thought he would have had no bother getting a quine. But he had been moping about your Kathleen all this time she had been married and borne you a son, little Brian, with his mother's eyes and face, but his hair still in baby curls the colour of straw, so that you couldn't tell if it would be black like his mother's hair.

So things had come to a crisis with Bryce in his celibacy and he takes a funny notion in his head that he might have your Kathleen after all, which you thought was strange in a bloke who had never envied anything you had before, and was always readier to give than to take away. Queer how things take shape in folk's minds and it is sometimes years before you realize what they have been up to behind your back.

Bryce arrived on his motor bike one fine Sunday afternoon,

just about the time you was down at the farm, feeding a calf or something, and for nearly an hour Bryce had Kathleen all to himself, whispering sweet nothings in her dainty ears, while little Brian played on the mat or ran outside to the neighbours. So here was you with a brimming pail of water, coming up the brae to the cottar houses, 'cause you never liked to come home empty-handed when you was passing the water tap down at the farm, for all of it had to be carried up the hill. Your little son comes running down the brae to meet you, his baby-fat legs wobbling under his growing weight, though he doesn't have the sense to tell you there was a stranger with mummy, which might have put you on your guard or aroused your suspicion of Bryce. So you takes your little boy by the hand, on the other side from the water pail, walking up the hill, and you pass the time of day with the foreman, Badgie Summers, who is sitting on the grass by the side of the farm road, reading the Sunday paper, his teenage dother beside him, Oslena, her that always gave you the glad eye at the week-ends, when she came home from the place she was fee-ed at, and would have had you away from Kathleen in no time if you had given her any encouragement. And there she was, staring at you with her green-grey eyes as round as marbles, smiling cheek-ily, her brown hair in curlers under a headsquare, with dabs of rouge on her cheeks, her lips like ripe strawberries, her thin skirt well above her dimpled knees, stockingless and wearing her mother's carpets, home for the day with her parents. She gets up and grabs your bairn in the passing and soon has him on the grass, tickling the life out of him while he squeals with laughter. Then you spies this big motor bike standing in the close, with a helmet and leather gloves lying on the saddle-tank, and you couldn't guess who it might belong to. You leave your pail of water in the porch and walks through to the kitchen, and here is Bryce at tea with your wife and she pours you a cup when you sat down at the table.

Of course you was pleased to see your old school pal, almost shook hands with him, though it isn't much done among working folks: you just say 'Aye aye, fit like?' and he says 'Nae bad; fit like yersel'?' and you say 'Fine!' and you are off to a flying start. You said you couldn't think who the motor bike belonged to, and Bryce said he had just bought it second-hand from a dealer in Brochan, though it was only a year old and in fine fettle, and that he'd like to take you for a run on the pillion. You thought maybe he wanted to take Kathleen out; but no, that wasn't his plan apparently and it was you he wanted. You was only being evil minded and suspicious, because you minded how he used to look at her before you was married. It was a shame to think such things of Bryce and it was good of him to come and see you, which was more than some of your other pals had done and you felt pleased about it. So you newses away about not much in particular, mostly the weather and how you liked to work at Kingask, seeing you had been there a couple of months now. For all his good points Bryce was a deep thinker and you felt you could never get to the bottom of him, what with his half sniggering smile and sly poking humour you was never sure if he was taking the raise of you or no, though he was always friendly and good-hearted and had never done you an ill turn since you had played together as bairns on your father's place in the Bog-side.

For nearly an hour you blethered and Bryce said he had some-times looked for Kathleen and you up at his father's place. But you reminds him that you don't have a motor bike and side-car for the wife and bairn; that you couldn't afford such a thing, only push bikes, and that Tilliehash (his father's farm) wasn't all that handy for a bus, so he said he would come and meet you with the gig if you thought about it. He said he had just come down for a run on his new bike to see how you was getting on, and that Kathleen looked bonnier than ever and that the bairn was fair growing he thought for all the short time it seemed since you was married, and he gave Brian a half-crown for his piggy bank. But you wasn't all that keen to go for a ride on his pillion, because you wasn't dressed and it was your Sunday on duty at the farm. But Bryce wouldn't take no for an answer and he said it wouldn't take long for you to change your breeks and you would be back again before cow time.

You couldn't think why Bryce was so anxious to have you on his motor bike, unless it was to show you how fast it could go – a big 500cc Norton with the new saddle-tank, twin-port exhausts as clear as a sixpence and twist-grip throttle control; silver streak you might have called it shining there in the sun. Bryce put on his helmet and gloves and adjusted his goggles and pushed the big bike off the stand, wheeling it to the gable at the roadside. Kathleen came to the gable-end to see you off, with little Brian by the hand, and Badgie Summers had gone inside with his daughter for their afternoon cup of tea. You got on the pillion behind Bryce and he stood on the kick-start until the huge bike snorted into motion, then slipped in the clutch and moved off slowly down the brae, while you lifted your feet to the foot-rests and held on to Bryce round the waist, your face sheltered from the wind by his helmet, and under you the throb of the bike like a powerful horse that you rode smoothly without a gallop. 'What do ye think of her than?' Bryce shouted back at you over his shoulder, once you was on the main road and he had opened her up, the wind whipping at his words. You had put on your cap back to front in case you might lose it in the wind. 'Oh grand,' you cried out; 'just grand!' trying to please him, and to make him feel you was impressed, and yet not wanting to start a conversation at such speed, for you felt sure Bryce was trying to scare you to death or give you the thrill of your life on his big new motor cycle. The sea was a speeding strip of blue on your right, and on your left the farms and crofts and cottages like punctuation marks that measured the speed you were going; flying like a bird, except in the villages, where Bryce snorted her down with the twist-grip on the handlebars – then off again, up hill and down dale like a switch-back, through Badengour and along the narrow road to the cliff-tops, where Bryce stopped and both of you got off and he stanced his bike on a patch of sand and pebble.

You was just beginning to enjoy it and wondered why Bryce had stopped so soon; for if he had wanted to give you a real joy-ride he should have gone further, taken you for a long detour inland, a round-about way for getting home, giving you a chance to see the country. But that was not his intention apparently and though you was a little displeased you didn't say anything; after all the bike was his and he could go where he pleased, you was only his passenger. Bryce removed his gloves and goggles and put them in the pockets of his leather coat, but kept on the small helmet that was fastened by a strap under his chin, then the two of you sauntered off in the direction of the towering cliffs, the cry of the gulls getting louder as you approached. It was past the gull egg season and you wondered what Bryce had brought you here for, unless it were to enjoy the grandeur of the scene, where a lot of young gulls were on the wing, like white sparrows at such dizzy heights, diving down from the cliff face and levelling out smoothly above the greenish waters, then rising again with a scream of triumph that echoed against the cliff walls. Although you had never actually been here before you knew something of the history of the place: the saga of Dundarg castle for instance, and the early settlements of the flint-knappers, long before the Picts – but Hell's Lum you had never heard of and that was what Bryce wanted to show you. It was a massive cavern with only a small crack on the cliff top where you could just squeeze inside and listen to the waves in ceaseless turmoil in some mysterious subterranean passage far underfoot. It was like the noise of distant thunder, frightening in its mystery, while you tried to imagine the convulsion of water that made that dreadful noise, struggling far inland under the cliffs, thudding against a prison of rock, black and fathomless, where the sea had entered from a small cave at high tide. You both stood inside the fizzure of Hell's Lum, the cold draught from the flue hitting your faces while you peered over the edge, tilting the cap on your head, while you stared down the black chute to hell's cauldron, though you couldn't see anything in the darkness beyond the ledge of rock. Nor was it really dangerous, as further passage was blocked by a huge rock at the entrance, with only a tiny crack where a man might squeeze through with difficulty, or someone could push you through in a struggle to almost certain death beyond. Bryce said it had been used by the smugglers in the old days, when they entered the cave at low tide and unloaded their boats on the rock shelves, then hauled their booty up the lum or rock chimney with ropes to the ledge where you was standing, most likely tobacco, rum and brandy, then carried it off in the night when all good excisemen were supposed to be in bed. It was all very interesting and of course you knew something of the caves yourself on this cliff girt coastline, though you had never seen them, especially the Hermit's Cave and that of Lord Slypigo, where he had concealed himself after Culloden, hiding from the Redcoats, while the peasantry on his estate brought him food and drink in secret, in peril of their lives, though none would betray him. He was afraid to go near his castle (now a ruin near Spitullie) which had been seized and guarded by the Government, and you had been told he had hid himself in the house where you was born; a thackit biggin' with stone-clay walls, under the box bed, which was timbered up and wallpapered, while the searching Redcoats jabbed the chaff mattress with their bayonets though they never found him. All this you told Bryce, while the pair of you cowered back from the black abyss and the awful thunder that trembled the cliff under your feet. And maybe your telling of it took your pal's mind from more serious intent, like pushing you into Hell's Lum – but maybe his courage had failed him.

Outside the sun was shining, and far out in the thin haze you could just make out the hills or Paps of Caithness, shimmering on the misty blue horizon across the Moray Firth. You wandered along the cliff top and then the two of you sat down on the spine grass, smoking your pipes and gazing out to sea, where here and there a fishing boat laboured on the waves, bound for Brochan or Candlebay. Was Bryce still thinking of Kathleen? He had become so suddenly quiet watching the sea, his thoughts far away while he puffed at his pipe; not a word between you, both staring into space. But the devil was working overtime in his mind, scheming how to be rid of you without trace so that Bryce could have your wife. Of course you never suspected this. It was long afterwards when you looked in the mirror of life and you saw an action replay; when you fitted all the pieces together that the jig-saw became clear.

Right now you never realized the danger you was in and you was taken by surprise. You just couldn't make out what had come over Bryce to take off your cap and throw it in the air, whirling in the wind towards the cliff tops. Now he stood over you without a smile on his face, stern as rock; pipe in hand, a challenge in his eyes. You stood up beside him, while he put his pipe in his breast pocket, and you realized you couldn't do the same to him, the leather helmet strapped tightly under his chin. If it was meant as a joke you couldn't return it. 'What was that for?' you asked, surprised by the stern, half mocking look on his face. 'I bet ye wunna climb down for it,' he said, while you put your pipe away and stared towards your checked cap tilting in the wind on the cliff edge. It had just failed to go over and lay on a green slope overhanging the water. Maybe he was just bluffing but you would try to get your cap back; if he thought you was scared you would make a damned good try to prove him wrong. Maybe you should have been less hot headed and asked him to retrieve your cap; after all it was him who threw it away and he should have to bring it back. That was only fair. But it was a challenge and you had accepted it. Bryce was testing your courage, like he sometimes did at school; daring you to reach for the cap, and as you slithered down the slope he came after you, but stayed at a safe distance. Your cap lay on a grassy slope just beyond reasonable hand-grasp, where the cliff edge overhung the sea, the white green waves swirling underneath and the young gulls screaming in beautiful ballet on the eddying wind, dipping and rising gracefully above the swell of the sea. Bryce came a bit nearer, sidling down the slope, his leather jerkin open in the breeze, while you tip-toed nearer the cliff edge; now on the slope that was like standing on a barrel, rolling towards the sea. The sky was a hotch-potch of white and smoky cloud patch, the sea a surge of white green water, the wind from the cliff-top ruffling your hair over your eyes, while you straddled the barrel of stone, nearer and nearer the giddy edge.

You couldn't stand any longer and got down on your knees, then lay flat on your belly, crawling towards the cap, your arm outstretched to reach it – now at your fingertips, ever so close; one more shove forward on your belly, with the shout of Bryce in your ears: 'Come back,' he cried, 'never mind the bonnet, let it go – I'll buy ye a new ane!' He had lost his nerve and couldn't do it. At the last moment his courage had failed him and he couldn't push you over. He couldn't come near enough to give you the final shove. You had crawled beyond his reach. If he had got you on a sheer edge he might have tried it, but not on this sloping barrel. Still he shouted but you wasn't turning back now; not with the cap at your fingernails, lying on a patch of daisies and crow-foot anemone, scrabbling at the stone and sea-grass with your free hand, an anchor for your body on the overhang. You had disturbed the gulls and they screamed over your head in confusion; Bryce still shouting, your arm at full length, the diced cap tilting to your touch, your body writhing on the crumbling edge of earth and pebble. But now you had it, your cap firmly in your eager grasp, and you edged your way back up the grassy slope to sanity.

Bryce grabbed your arm and pulled you up the slope, thankful it seemed that you hadn't gone over the edge. 'I couldna have done that tae save my life,' he said calmly. 'Ye've mair guts than I thocht!' Of course you never suspected him at the time and thought it was all a silly joke that had nearly misfired; a challenge maybe to test your courage and you had won. Bryce had done that sort of thing at school and sometimes you had lost, taunting you to tears almost over it, and then he would treat you to a bar of chocolate and all was well again. But this time the prank seemed more sinister; more contrived, with some evil purpose behind it you couldn't yet understand. But you told him it was a damned silly thing to do all the same; risking your life like that for nothing. He said he didn't mean to throw your cap so far, but that the wind caught it and took it nearer the edge than he intended. You could have come back when he shouted he said: there was no need for you risking your neck like that for a bludy bonnet and you shouldn't have taken it so seriously, even though it was a challenge. But Bryce had a curious sense of fun you thought and mostly at your expense. But now he was in better spirits than he had been all afternoon: thankful perhaps that his ill-hatched crime had not been committed; that he had thrust the devil behind him, or at least thwarted his evil purpose, and that he could face the world again with a free conscience.

You brushed the sand and grit from your clothes and Bryce adjusted his goggles and put on his leather gloves again. The pair of you got on the big motor bike and Bryce stood with all his weight on the kick-start, wurting the twist-grip while he paddled it on to the road, slipped in the gear and you were off, purring back along the coast road to Kingask. The wind was in your back but colder now; the sun a white disc in the western sky, but still time to spare before cow time. Bryce dropped you off at the cottage but wouldn't come inside. Perhaps he couldn't face Kathleen again but said he had promised to be back home before tea time.

Not until Bryce was away on his bike, and Kathleen and you were alone in the house after tea, and she told you how Bryce had tempted her while you was away at the farm – not until then did you begin to suspect him, and then only partially because it seemed so ridiculous. Bryce had asked Kathleen how she would like to be a farmer's wife instead of a cottar, turning out his pocket-book and showing her wads of paper money, comparing his well-to-do position with your comparative poverty. But Kathleen had merely smiled at him and said that money could never come between her and her marriage. She was embarrassed beyond measure she said and glad to see you pass the window on your return from the farm. She said you had come back at the right time or he might have gone a bit further.

Maybe some day you would tell Kathleen of your experience on the cliff-top; once you had figured it all out. But not now; you wasn't ready for it yet, and you didn't want to give Kathleen an ill opinion of Bryce. Oh that was just like him you said, always wanting to impress folk; he had always been like that, even at school, but only joking really. Maybe it was all mere chance and coincidence; yet so neatly contrived that time put a seal of truth on it, or at least a measure of probability, and you was sure the devil had a hand in it.

And it was just possible you could have fallen off the cliff by accident, reaching for your cap, while Bryce flew for assistance on his motor bike, telling everybody (including Kathleen) that you had gone too near the edge. There was nobody to contradict him. The perfect crime, and maybe he could have had your Kathleen after all.

But it is a fact that Bryce Holt never came to visit you and Kathleen again, not in all his life; nor have you seen him since and he died a bachelor.

Dockenbrae

Old Sally Birse of Dockenbrae had never been the same body since the place was burned down a couple of years back. She aye thought she heard the howling of the nowt in the burning byres and sometimes she had the nightmare over it and wakened her man with her screaming. Folk said that old Magnus Birse had set fire to the place himself to get the insurance money to build a new steading and re-stock his byres, and that it served him right if his old woman took the nightmare over it and kept him from his sleep. But outsiders always said something of that sort if a fairmtoon was burned down and maybe they were just lucky that it didn't happen to themselves. But old Magnus had got his new steading in spite of them and was back on his feet again with a fine new herd of fat nowt and a puckle swine forbye.

But if you looked in by at Dockenbrae at a dinner time you might see the old wife making her water in a brander by the kitchen door, holding up her skirts a bit and letting it run down her legs into her high-laced boots. And if the kitchie quine didn't get a clatcht on old Sally she would hyter down to the stable door to give the men their orders for the afternoon. Otherwise Tom Buyers that was the new grieve would put two fingers in his mouth and whistle for old Magnus, who would emerge from some hold or bore about the steading and take his wife to the farmhouse, out of sight of the men folk.

But in her young day Sally Birse had been a different woman and wore the breeks folk said and kept Magnus in a tight corner. It was nothing new for her to give the men their orders at yoking time, and if Magnus said something she didn't like she soon spoke up. The men didn't like it either, taking orders from a woman, and they sometimes wondered if she had grown a stroop, seeing there were no bairns about the place, for maybe she had changed her sex. Nowadays Sally never got the length of the stable but pished herself or she was clear of the kitchen door, something to do with her nerves since the fire folk said, that she wasn't like that before. All the lads were new at the Term anyway, 'cause Magnus had a clean toon when the old grieve left; but they had heard about Sally in her young day though there was no doubt about her sex when they saw her over the brander.

Since all the cottars were new it took a while to size each other up and for their bairns to get acquainted; some of them wondering if they had come from the hay to the heather, from the clover to stubble, or if old Magnus was as black a devil as he was painted, or if his wife was as dottled as they said she was. And Magnus had notions too, thinking that maybe he had fee-ed the wrong lad for second-horseman, because he wouldn't take in his pair from the grass park to be ready at yoking time, neither in the morning nor at noon (not that he slept-in mind you, for he was always there on time) but just sat on the cornkist smoking his pipe and kicking the wooden box with his heels or yoking time, while the other lads harnessed their beasts for grubber, harrows, or rollers, drill-plough or dung cart.

Then, if it were noon, and just about the time that old Sally came out to the brander, Runcie Smart would loup from his cornkist, take a few cubes of oil-cake from under the lid, his halter ropes from the forestalls, and away he'd go, whistling for his mares, a pair of dapple greys that had survived the fire and were the pride of the countryside; better than Buyers' pair (him being foreman as well as grieve) and it caused a bit of jealousy between the two of them – that the second lad should have a better pair of horses than the foreman.

So Runcie got hold of his pair, just inside the gate, where they were waiting for him and the handful of cattle cake that Runcie had stolen for them, never troubling to run off while he slipped the thin rope through the iron ring on their halters and led them through the white clover to the gate. But this was after yoking time, when the foreman and the loon were pulling out of the stable with their horses fully harnessed, ready for a yoking's wark, while Runcie still had to harness his beasts and give them the chance of a drink at the horse trough.

In her young day Sally Birse would have spoken to Runcie Smart right quick about this breach of contract; which was what you might have called it, though it was never in writing, but

104

a customary habit among the horsemen of the Bogside, and the farmers believed from long tradition that they had a right to expect such service. But Sally never got half-way to the stable or somebody grabbed her, or even yet she might have told Runcie what she thought of him and his foreign ways, for Runcie was a man from the Mearns and not accustomed to Buchan ways; though some said he was just being downright thrawn because he didn't like Buyers and wanted to pick a quarrel with him. Old Magnus didn't say anything to Runcie but he put Buyers up to it; loading the gun as you might say while Buyers was expected to fire it, and thus stand the consequences if it back-fired, though Magnus never expected that it would.

So Buyers spoke to Runcie and told him right sharply to have his horse in the stable by yoking time. But Runcie up and tells him he will do nothing of the sort; that down in the South a man never haltered his pair or yoking time and he wasn't going to start it here, just because the Buchan farmers were such greedy lads for wark. They nearly came to blows about it; Runcie like a wee bantam cock and Buyers a big bubblie-jock with his tail fanned out and his wings trailing on the ground, sparring round each other in the close and the feathers like to fly from tooth and claw. Runcie took his pipe from his mouth in case it got broke and dared Buyers with his stickit nieve. So Buyers went away in a sulk, muttering something about letting old Magnus do his ain dirty work. But he must have told Magnus the upshot of the thing because at the end of the month when the cottars got their pay Magnus gave Runcie the sack and told him to get out of his cottage.

So that was that and Buyers the grieve was fair cock-a-hoop about getting rid of Runcie Smart, and having a laugh with the other billies and saying how hard it would be for Runcie to get another cottar job six weeks after the May term.

The hyowe was just started, when everybody that wasn't there got their character, or 'their kale through the reek,' as they said, from the Laird himsel' to Joe Meeks, the tramp that went with the threshing mills and sleepit in the barns 'cause he had lice. And Runcie wasn't spared: 'The cocky wee crater,' as Buyers called him, seeing he wasn't there to defend himself. So you got real friendly with Buyers, and though you was only the loon

105

about the place he was right glad to have you on his side (or so he believed) whatever the others thought, though one of them was your own father, hoeing at the other end of the squad. Head cattleman he was and you was second cattleman and orra-beaster (working the odd horse) besides looking after two colts and the shelt you drove for old Magnus and his mistress in the Governess cart, a small gig with rubber tyres and cushioned side seats, used by the gentry in the old days to drive their Governess around their estates with the bairns.

Tom Buyers was the first man you had ever seen smoking tea-leaves. His wife rationed him to two ounces of black twist (Bogie Roll) a week, and if this were exhausted before the grocer's vanman returned the following week he had to resort to the tea-caddy on the mantelshelf. It wasn't pleasant smoking: rather hot and tasteless, so that he slivered down his pipe stem and there was always a bead of moisture hanging from the bowl, and she raged at him for that, something he had to put up with from being hen-pecked.

Runcie Smart swore out that Buyers was afraid of his wife. She was a bit younger than Buyers and known as the Flower of Mull-den, where she came from, though you couldn't say why they called her that. She was no special beauty, in fact the opposite, with moose-coloured hair and never a smile on her face; plain and childless and rather sulky, with little to say to her neighbours, which maybe wasn't a bad thing biding in a cottar hoose.

But she had bonnie legs, and all the men looked at them, with a wink to each other if Buyers wasn't aside, and they agreed you wouldn't see the likes of them on anybody but a film star.

Old Magnus engaged a single lad to take Runcie's place. His folk had a croft just across the parks on the moss road and he went home on his bicycle for all his food, so that he was no bother to Sally Birse or her serving quine.

The hyowe was finished and the hay in the cole and some of the peats home but Runcie Smart was still in his thackit biggin'. Maybe Buyers had been right: that Runcie couldna get a job atween the Terms; but some said he wasn't looking for one, just sitting in his hovel to spite old Magnus. Nobody knew what he lived on though some said he had applied for Parish Relief. His wife had two bairns at her hip and one in her oxter; yet Runcie

106

was no thief, nor was he much of a poacher. In fact the farming folk had nearly forgotten about Runcie Smart and his predicament when old Magnus gets a lawyer's letter sueing for a year's wages for Runcie, besides the cash value of his perquisites and the right to stay in his cottage until the next May Term. Furthermore, the letter said that he, Magnus Birse, had dismissed his worker without proper cause: that since there was no written agreement of policy there had been no breach of contract, or words to that effect, and that the alternative to the forgoing was to reinstate the said employee in his former employment, otherwise further proceedings would be taken in court.

It was a stamagaster for old Magnus, and when he showed the letter to his wife she pee-ed herself, never getting the length of the brander, but let it go on the flagstoned floor of the kitchen, where the quine had to dry it up with the sack cloth.

Magnus put on his spectacles again and came down the close with the letter to Buyers, like a squirrel with a nut, for he always trotted about like a beast on its hind legs, bent forward with his hands in front, palms inward, like paws, gnarled with rheumatism and grasping the letter. Buyers had been glad to get rid of Runcie, because you might say Runcie was undermining his authority as grieve about the place; the man not doing what he was told, which was an unwritten law of the farming hierarchy, that a worker must be disciplined, like he was in the army almost, or get out of his tied cottage. But the letter changed his tune and Magnus had an accusing look behind those thick glasses. Buyers could sense it even before the old man spoke: blaming him for picking a quarrel with Runcie over nothing and causing all this trouble with the man. Buyers had a look on his face like a cwe in a dipping trough and it looked like he would go into a sulk.

Magnus said they would just have to take Runcie back; that he had no choice, because he couldn't afford to pay a whole year's wages for nothing, besides the lad who was taking Runcie's place. They would just have to take Runcie back as orraman until the November Term, when they could get rid of the single man and Runcie could have his horses back, if he would agree to it. So old Magnus had to go crawling to Runcie's door telling him to come back, even to asking his favour to accept the job as orraman until the Term, when he could have his horse team again.

So Runcie came back with the buckles on his wall-tams shining like new silver and a gloss on his boots like newly ploughed lea, smoking a new Stonehaven pipe, and sets himself up on the corn-kist again, like a dethroned monarch back in his royal chair, banging away with his heels to the tune of 'Drumdelgie'. Fair Cock o' the Walk he was and like to rule the roost at Docken-brae, watching the single billie taking in his dapple greys from the grass park before yoking time to have them harnessed on the dot, never letting on if he would have done the same, though it isn't likely when he had a lawyer at his back.

The corn was unsheathed, though still a bit green, expected to rax another six inches before it was fully ripe. The hay was all in the stack and forbyes a yoking in the horse shim or a dab at the second-hoe you was mostly employed in the peat moss.

The chaumer at Dockenbrae had been burned in the fire two years earlier, and when they built the new steading they didn't plan for a new one, as there were plenty of cottar houses for married men on the place. When you came to Dockenbrae as a halflin it was agreed that you got your board and bed with your parents, seeing that your old man was cattleman. It had been a fine change from the chaumer life and you got a better diet from your ain mither than you was accustomed to in the fairm kitchies, though Magnus paid her only a shilling a day for your keep, besides extra milk, tatties and oatmeal, and a load or two of peat for fuel.

Now your old man always took in the kye for the milking, three or four milk cows with the bull, a big black brute of an Aberdeen-Angus that Magnus hired out to the crofters round about who couldn't afford to keep one to serve their cows. He charged them so much for every calf and they had to pay your old man a shilling for every service with the bull, though it was only to open the gate to let them into the park. So it was no shilling no service as far as the crofters and your old man was concerned, though most of them paid up, especially if it was in the evening when they had to get your old man away from the fireside. Sex has no trysts in the bovine world and has to be answered on call, and folk had never heard of Artificial Insemination or 'glass tube calves' as they are called nowadays. Like the tenant farmer who had engaged an ex-fisherman as stockman and one day he had to send him with a cow in season to the Home Farm for service where the bull was kept. So the fisherman took the cow in a halter to the Home Farm, and when he returned the farmer thought he'd better ask him what had taken place, seeing that the fisherman lacked experience in these affairs with cattle.

'And foo did ye get on than?' the farmer asked when the fisherman entered the farm close with the cow.

'Oh fine,' said the fisherman. 'The bull went up beside the cow and whispered something in her lug, and for fear that she forgot what it was he wrote it on to her arse with a red pencil!'

Another version of the story was that when the farmer asked what had happened the fisherman replied simply: 'Oh top hole sir!' without a smile on his face.

'Och,' said the farmer, less convinced: 'I thocht you wad mak' an arse of it somewye!'

But old Magnus Birse kept a bull himself, so that your old man didn't have to go stravagin' over the countryside embarrassin' folk with sex starved cows. But between times, to keep the bull content, besides having him near at hand, he went to pasture with the milk herd, and he stood in a stall in the byre while his wives were being milked; chained by the neck to the forestall, though he also had a brass ring in his nostrils for emergencies, fixed there by the blacksmith – if you could get hold of it in any tussle you was likely to have with a frisky bull. The done thing was to chain the bull first, maybe with a bit of cotton-cake in the trough to take up his attention, then tie up the cows, while they chewed the cud and flapped their big lugs in your face, and you whispered their pet names and anything else you was feared to mention to the kitchicdccm in a haystack.

Like the farm cheil who was a bit shy and rather slow in the uptak' and didn't know what to say to his lass when he went courting. So he eavesdropped on a courting couple behind a hedge and listened to their conversation, especially concerning what the lad had to say. 'You have eyes like a dove,' says the lover, poetically, speaking in English to charm his lass, or to impress her with his refined vocabulary – 'You have eyes like a dove my dear; a breath like a thousand meadows . . . and you're a cupid!'

Next time our farming billy was out with his kitchie quine he sets her down in the hedge and says: 'Ye've een like a dog . . . a breath like a thoosand middens . . . and ye bugger ye're stupid!' And we can only guess the reaction of the offended maiden.

Ah well, one summer evening, when your old man bent down to pick up the bull's chain he turned on your father and threw him into the forestall, where he sat helpless in the cement trough while the great head of the bull played punch-ball with his knees, bashing them against the concrete, till his knee-caps seemed like egg-yolks with every yark from the muscled neck of the bull. It was a cat and mouse affair, the beast now roaring and foaming at the mouth, your old man at his mercy, while the great black mass of bone and muscle hurled itself against the figure jammed in the feed trough, crying for help, while the enraged bull, cheated of his fun of throwing him in the air, bellowed in his fury.

But wherever old Magnus was he heard the uproar, and he ran to the cow byre as fast as his tottering old legs would carry him. He opened the sliding door and saw what was happening, while your old man yelled from the forestall. Magnus grabbed a long-handled fork and jabbed at the bull. He was an old man over seventy, frail and bent with the years, but desperation gave him courage and he pricked at the tough hide of the sweating, bellow-ing animal; the warm smell of him strong in the byre, and the green skitter flying from the arse of him, his long tail lashing it all over the place. Magnus probed and stabbed at the black noisy brute till he fair danced in his frenzy, blowing and snorting from his brass-ringed nostrils, distended in rage, swack on his hoofs for his great size, till he pranced out of the stall and turned on his owner, while your old man crawled to the open door, through between the farmer's legs to safety, while Magnus held the beast at bay with the fork.

The cows stood around in wonder but never got in the way; perhaps a bit surprised at the onslaught of their chief on a human body. But Magnus stood his ground, prodding the sharp three-pronged fork at the bull, a valuable beast moneywise but a killer in his present mood; only the cold sharp steel held him off, or he would have crushed the old farmer as a fly against the wall. Magnus held the enraged beast at the end of his trident, like St George with the Dragon, his breath now coming in gasps from his efforts to defend himself. But he slipped and fell on the wet

110

greep and the bull lowered his head to charge. He was a coward against the cold steel, but now that the fork was down he gave Magnus a buffet that sent him along the greep like a bairn's toboggan, right between the legs of Runcie Smart in the open door, where he had dropped his milk flagon when he heard the noise.

Runcie ran past the bull, picked up the fork and thrust it into the animal's ribs, the brute now roaring in pain and terror, while Runcie withdrew the fork and dodged behind him. The fork was tipped with blood and there was a red trickle from the bull's ribs. He turned on Runcie but shied at the fork, and with a final snort he ran to mingle with the cows. Runcie opened the barn door and chased him inside, where he charged at the straw and threw it over his back.

Old Magnus had struggled to his feet and was groping in the straw and sharn for his glasses, lost in his tussle with the bull. Runcie went to your old man in the passage, now moaning in his agony and hugging his bruised knees. Runcie lifted him on to his feet but he couldn't stand. Magnus found his splintered glasses and stuck them on his nose again, grumbling about Buyers not being at hand at a time like this. It was a wonder he hadn't heard the commotion he said, while Runcie now tied up the cows. The kitchie quine came in with her pails for the milking, fair surprised at the uproar and staring at your old man lying in the passage. Magnus asked her if she had seen Buyers and she said he was over at the kitchen door with his teem flagon, waiting for his milk.

Runcie told Magnus your old man was crippled and couldn't stand on his legs, so he went off to tell Buyers to yoke the shelt in the float and take your old man home. So they laid him on the float, on a cushion of straw, still trembling in his fright of the bull, and they drove him gently down the cart road to the cottar house, where your mither was watching anxiously from the door.

You was sent to the village on your bike for the doctor. He came quickly in his motor car and looked at your old man and said that no bones were broken but that one of his knee-caps was dislocated and the other grazed and inflamed, besides severe bruising on his legs and shock. He was put to bed and the doctor said he would have to rest for a week or two and then try walking on crutches, which he would loan him from the surgery.

Magnus had the bull destroyed. A motor float came and took the brute away, and a gie struggle the driver had loading him, with a spring-hook fastened to the ring in his nostrils, with a long rope down the length of the byre to the loading ramp, up the gangway of the float, and out through a slot at the side, where the driver could pull on the rope when Buyers and Runcie loosened the bull, prodding him from behind with forks. But the brute was thrawn and lay down on the rope, staring about him with his bloodshot eyes, blowing and snorting and the sharn all over his back from his swinging tail. Buyers shouted in his ears and they got him to rise, twisting his tail and prodding with the forks till they got him on the gangway, then into the float and a chain about his neck – away to the slaughterhouse, his wives grazing contentedly by the wayside.

Your old man was a long time or he recovered from his pounding, and sometimes you wondered if he did recover completely. Physically he wasn't bad, except for a jab of rheumatics in his knees, when he could tell you it was going to rain. But his nerves were shattered, and he sometimes sat up in the night with a great yowl, till he wakened himself, and everybody else in the hoose, unless your mither got a dig at him with her elbow when he started, choking the scream in his throat, and when she asked what ailed him he said: 'It was that bull again wuman, he'll be the death o' me yet!'

But as far as Magnus was concerned there wasn't a man about the place like Runcie Smart. After all he had probably saved the old man's life, for if he hadn't appeared when he did, and acted so gamely, there's no saying what the bull would have done to old Magnus.

When the hairst was by it wasn't long or you could see that Buyers had watered all the corn rucks, seeing he had built them all himself and there was nobody else to blame. They were sprouting green round the shoulders by the middle of November, the sheaves all grown together so that they couldn't be thrashed and had to be thrown to the cattle as they were, a sore loss to old Magnus in his declining years. He was afraid to sack Buyers after what happened with Runcie Smart, but Buyers was that affronted he left of his own accord at the November Term. Runcie took his place and they kept on the single lad for the dapple greys. Runcie

112

had full charge at Dockenbrae until the roup in May, when Magnus sold everything off and bought a house in the village, a house with a new-fangled bathroom, where he had more control of his wife when she went looking for a brander by the kitchen door.

Dockenbrae was sold to another farmer and he never asked any of the old servants to stay on – not even the kitchie quine. He would be bringing new workers of his own choice to carry on the place and everybody at Dockenbrae had to look for other jobs.

Runcie Smart went home to a place about a dozen miles from Dockenbrae, in the next parish but one, where everybody was a stranger to him, or so he thought – but who should be foreman there but his old arch-enemy Tom Buyers. Each had engaged to the farmer without the other's knowledge, which was common enough, and as each was fee-ed on a twelve-month basis they would have had to put up with each other's company again for another whole year – such was the irony of the cottar's life.

Runcie's only consolation was the prospect of further admiring the leg-stems on the Flower o' Mullden, especially now that it was near the end of the nineteen-twenties and short skirts were the fashion with the women folk. And would you believe it – by the end of the twelve months Tom Buyers and Runcie Smart were as thick as fresh butter on oatcakes, each visiting the other, and Buyers' wife taking a great interest in Mrs Runcie's bairns, maybe because she had none o' her ain. And Runcie would be in by at Buyers' house of an evening, listening to his gramophone records, sitting by the fireside smoking their pipes, and when Buyers reached up for the tea-caddy Runcie would produce his pouch and offer him a pipeful of tobacco, the price he had to pay for inspiration from the Flower o' Mullden.

The Shearing

There was nothing extraordinary about the Monkshood place as a fairm toon; it looked like most of its neighbours in the Tully-marle countryside, hiding behind its muffler of trees, with only the lums of the dwallin' hoose showing in summer, though you could see most of the steading in winter when the trees were bare.

What was uncommon about the Monkshood farm was the man who owned and worked it, a retired doctor from London, who had done well in practice among the gentry there and came up north to fulfil a life's desire – a passion for farming. All his working life as a medical practitioner Dr Leiper had read and dreamed about having a farm of his own. The depression of the 'thirties had made it possible, when he came on holiday up north and the Monkshood place came on the market and nobody wanted to buy it; the price just right for his bank account with enough to spare to give him a reasonable start. It was a good farm the doctor had chosen, though more by chance than foresight or good judgement; land with a mixture of clay in the brown soil, especially on the upland parks that carried grass and turnips well, and even corn or barley in an average year when the sun didn't scorch the braes. There was some peat in the howes that needed to be drained for better cropping, but once he had the ditches cleaned he soon had them flushed with grass. There was also a lot of fencing to be done for the sheep he kept, and he bought a lot of new posts and wire and told the grieve to spare no expense in having the place secure, every post the same height and the wires level with the ground. Nor was he far from the peat moss, where he could supply himself and his workers with ample fuel, and faith he thought it a blessing in the cold batter of the north wind that came over the knowes in winter, whipping out of a freezing sky that sent the old doctor to warm himself at the kitchen range.

Dr Leiper's wife had died before his retirement, poor soul, worn out with cancer, though some folk just called it decline, leaving the doctor and their son Kenneth in the care of the housekeeper, a Miss Biper, who had been in their service for a two three years. Young Kenneth was now nearing twenty-three and sitting for a degree in science at the college in Aberdeen. Miss Biper had moved up north with the doctor, complaining bitterly about the coldness of the weather and the infernal rain that was never far away; and the thick damp fog that came rolling up from the sea and hid everything for days on end, so that she couldn't see the wee cottar house at the end of the farm road where the grieve lived, nor any of her farming neighbours, whether they had a washing out or no, which was most unlikely in the seeping mist. Maybe she had been a bit sheltered down in London yonder and felt a bit cosier, and London fogs didn't isolate a body as they did up here; there was always the neighbours and the houses across the street, the odd bit of gossip at the shops and the bus stop. Nowadays Miss Biper had to rely on the local vanman for almost everything she required, and any tittle-tattle that was going in the district. When she went to Aberdeen she had to take the country bus, a long weary lumbering journey with very seldom anybody to talk to that she knew, and very little in the scenery that inspired her urban mind. All this because the doctor didn't have a motor car, and hired a local taxi to take him about on his farming affairs.

And there was that domineering fog-horn on the coast that moaned most of the night, so that she couldn't go to sleep for its monotony, and the whole dark world seemed to be closing in upon her little bed. Of course the neighbours never believed this when the vanman told them, for they were sure she was more often in the doctor's double bed than she was in her own single one, creeping ben to him when he wanted her, the lamp in her hand, and if you was calving a cow about the place or lambing a ewe in the dark hours of spring you could see what you thought was going on, though up till now nobody had managed to prove it. Willie Bartok that was the grieve had the lambing in the springtime, sleeping time about with his assistant in the farm house, one relieving the other in the lambing buchts, and they said they heard the housekeeper talking in the doctor's room

115

when she was supposed to be in her own. But Miss Biper was good to the men and they wouldn't breathe a word against her, unless it were behind their hand so to speak, or over a friendly pint at the Emporium; and if Willie Bartok reached the stage of blowing the froth from his tumbler he would tell you there was more in the bitch than anybody was aware of, except the doctor maybe who knew her better. Aye faith Willie said he had seen something uncanny at the Monkshood place; something that made him wonder, but the doctor was a gentleman and he wasn't saying another ill word on the pair of them.

Be all that as it may, in daylight hours you would never have suspected anything irregular between Dr George Leiper and his housekeeper, for he treated her with the utmost respect, always addressing her as 'Miss Biper', as if he had never been nearer to her than across the dinner table. Norma was her christian name but he was never heard to use it in such familiarity, and she always approached him as 'Mr Leiper', not 'Doctor' Leiper as you might have expected, him being a specialist and all that. But Bella the kitchie quine had sharp eyes and sharper ears, and as Miss Biper kept her pretty well in her place (mostly in the kitchen) she wasn't slack to find fault with her employers, or to slander them a bit if she got the least inkling of their intimacy.

But the doctor was well liked in the parish, especially by the crofters round about who borrowed some of his implements from time to time from the grieve, who first asked the doctor if so and so could have the Tumbling Tom for a turn at his hay, or the horse lorry for a load of straw? In the first years, before the doctor got to know his neighbours, he would ask his grieve what sort of chap this neighbour billy was, and would he bring the thing back unharmed? So Willie Bartok spoke for the crofter lads with the doctor, who had the best and newest implements in the parish, and so long as they brought them back clean and un-damaged they could borrow what they wanted.

Though the doctor was well enough to do he never mixed with the bigger farmers or the gentry, always with the poorer folks (maybe because he had seen enough of the toffs in Harley Street) and some of the crofters and cottars would approach him with an ailment their own doctors couldn't cure. He would never visit a patient, in case he offended the local physician, but if a patient could be brought before him he would listen carefully to their symptoms and advise them on what they could do to help themselves. Some folk called him a 'Quack' for this while others he had helped said he could perform miracles, an allegation which brought him to the notice of the minister, the Rev. Pullock, down at the manse at Tullymarle, surrounded by his crows, where you couldn't get a shot at them so near the kirk and the graves, though they ravaged your tattie parks and sheltered in the manse trees. He was a bit like a crow himself the Rev. Pullock, dressed in his black surtoo coat and pedalling along on his bicycle, except for the dirty white collar round his neck. He paid the doctor a visit on his bicycle, not to bless him as a saint or for his powers of healing, but to see if he could get him to join his kirk, for the doctor would be a good source of revenue, especially if he could make him an elder. But the doctor was non-committal, merely indicating that he belonged to a brotherhood of his own choosing, and that most likely they would give him decent burial when the time came, though it wouldn't be in the kirkyard at Tullymarle.

The doctor kept a lot of sheep on the hill parks, a fine flock of Leicester Cheviots with a reputation for prize-taking and a pedigree for good breeding; strong heavy ewes that were a struggle when you compared them with the ewes of the neighbours who shared the doctor's dipping trough, because they couldn't afford one themselves, or hadn't taken the trouble to build one, what with the drainage problem and dripping slips and gathering pens and foot-rot troughs that were required to meet the new regulations demanded by the government. Of course they paid the doctor for the use of his trough and brought their own dip; even brought sticks and peat to heat the water to melt the pails of solid McDougal Sheep Dip, but for all the doctor charged them gave no inducement to have a dipping trough of their own.

The shearing was a bit late that year that young Kenneth Leiper was expected to pass his exams at the university. The doctor had spoken to his grieve about young Kenneth's homecoming, expressing a desire to see his son again and hoping that this time he would graduate and qualify for a teaching post in science, seeing he wasn't the least bit interested in agriculture.

Willie Bartok thought he knew young Kenneth fairly well,

though he'd been grown up before his father came north. A studious cheil you would have thought and serious like when he came home for the holidays and sometimes worked with the men at the hay or in the peat moss, or hyowing the neeps or tatties. But Willie the grieve knew there was another side to young Kenneth, a side that his father knew little about, except for the debts he sometimes had to pay for him, mostly gambling debts, though he told his old man a different story. The glaring fact was that young Kenneth had no interest whatsoever in his education, and his passion in life was drink and gambling, all the time hoodwinking his father with his good intentions, and how far the old man suspected him was anybody's guess. He had a bit lass too that he sometimes brought home with him, a better quine than he deserved; but she hadn't been seen for a while and folk thought he had given her the slip, or maybe she had left him for his bad habits.

Kenneth had bad drinking bouts and he kept bad company. More than once the grieve had come upon him in the barn, sleeping it off where his cronies had left him from a passing motor car, or when he stepped off a bus, all boozed up and afraid to meet the housekeeper or his father; and Willie Bartok would take him up the road in the darkness of morning to the cottar house, where his wife would wash young Kenneth's face, brush his hair and his suit and give him breakfast to sober him up a bit before he met his father, sometimes keeping him at the fireside till nearly dinner time. And there was those strange tablets he carried in his pocket that he said were to help him through his exams, and to help him look his father in the face with another failure.

Willie Bartok gathered his sheep early on the morning of the shearing, as soon as the dew was off their backs, the collie dog swinging round the brae to gather them in, rounding up mothers and lambs without a bark, simply answering to Willie's whistle from the gate, where he stood ready to open it when the flock had been foregathered. He would do the same with every park, for there were several flocks scattered on the braes, and Willie liked to have a flock gathered and penned for the shearers before breakfast, when the lambs would be separated from their mothers, the ewes herded to the catching pens to be brought before the shearers.

118

You could hear the baa-ing of the ewes on the neighbouring farms, and the persistent bleating of the lambs, now they were denied their mothers' teats, and the folk would say 'Faith aye, the doctor's at the shearin'!' A tarpaulin sheet was spread out upon the grass for the shearers to work on, mostly to keep the wool clean, while they sharpened their long shears on an oil stone, their pipes lighted and ready for the fray. They were hired men, mostly two of them, who made their living at the shearing, going from farm to farm in the summer months, and when that was finished they took to ditching or working in the peat moss; then harvest, and draining and fencing in the spring, casual work they did in their spare time from working on their small crofts that couldn't earn them a living. Dick Sow and Harry Hemp were men who could clip a ewe in about three-and-a-half to four minutes at the height of the season, when the wool had risen nearly an inch from the skin, with only the merest threads holding it, where the shearers made a quick and easy entrance, flashing round the falling fleece like hand-made lightning; snaking round the body of the ewe in a growing curve, the rich white wool falling back before the incessant clisp of steel, the blue bladed scissors slicing into the oily fleece while they held the ewe in the various positions that suited them, tilting their restive bodies this way and that, starting at the throat and finishing up at the tail, until they had them out of their coats and standing for a moment in the sun, breathing fast on a full stomach, and seemingly mesmerized in their nakedness, then leaping from the tarpaulin sheet with a new swiftness, bounding for their lambs and freedom. The ewes returned naked to the fold, so that the bairns scarcely knew their mothers, except for her baa and the feel of her teats, while they nosed her udder for suck, big growing lambs that were thirsty from the day's heat, bouncing their heads under the mother's flanks, lifting her nearly off her hind legs, a lamb at each side mostly, wagging their short tails gleefully, and the mothers sniffing over them in jollification that the worst was over and they were reunited with their bairns.

Two of the farm hands bundled up the fleeces, tying them separately for trampling into the woolsack, now slung from the rafters in the empty byre. Willie Bartok had a steady job driving away the shorn ewes and their lambs and bringing in another flock for clipping. The men who tied the fleeces took the ewes to the shearers, catching the ewes by the neck in the narrow pens with self-closing gates, worked with a thin rope and a weight over a post. They caught the struggling ewes and dragged them by the chin and flanks to the tarpaulin sheet, where they set them on their hunkers, each man a ewe at a time, and held them there until a shearer finished the ewe he was at and took over, splitting the wool at her throat and working down her belly, first round one side to her back and then the other side, peeling off her fleece like a jacket, even to the leg holes.

The shearers were paid for the number of ewes they clipped, each man counting his own by taking a penny from his pocket and dropping it into his cap on the grass, or by taking a match from one pocket and dropping it into another, each man using his own method. And there was no cheating, because the number of ewes they clipped had to correspond with the number of the flock, including bare-backs, ewes that had lost their wool on barbed wire fences or tufted over the whin bushes. But the shearers mostly snipped off the tufts that were left on their backs and counted her as a full fledged ewe they had clipped, helping themselves to a bonus they fully deserved. An average fleece weighed from five to seven pounds from the bigger ewes, and when trampled into the great woolsacks the total wool clip could reach up to nearly two tons.

The shearing lasted for three or four days, depending on the weather and how early in the forenoon the shearers could get started, sometimes waiting or the sun was hot, which brought out the oil on the wool, maybe giving you a bit more weight and making it easier to insert the shears between the wool and the skin of a ewe's back.

Now the kitchiedeem came over to the sheepfold with the piece basket, hot tea and scones with strawberry jam, biscuits and a bottle of beer for each man, thirsty at their work, tormented with heat and flies. So the shearers finished the ewe they were at and all work stopped for nearly half-an-hour, while the shepherds teased the quine about her lads and she poured their tea and took their banter in good spirit, sometimes returning it as good as she got. Even the bleating of the sheep died down, except for the occasional high-pitched baa from the grass pens where the lambs were still in orphanage. After tea the shepherds drank their beer and had their smoke and ground their shears on the oil-stone, counted their pennies or matchsticks and talked to Miss Biper, who had come over to see how the work was progressing, and maybe to crack a joke, even a blue one, for she wasn't above a hearty laugh was Miss Norma Biper, no matter what the cause of it. She had extra men to cook for during the shearing and she preferred doing it herself rather than leave it all to the kitchen lass.

After dinner the doctor appeared, a grey tweed hat on his head, a knee-length coat of mixed texture, even in the height of summer, breeches and topped socks and his walking cane, more out of habit than the need of one. He was clean shaven, rather puffy faced with high colouring and a bee-stung underlip, his eyes slightly bloodshot while he gazed on the flashing shears of the clippers and the growing mound of newly fallen fleeces. Sheep fascinated him, and what he had read about them in books he now endeavoured to put into practice, the ambition of a lifetime; all the years of work in the medical profession merely a means to an end, the realization of a dream, and he counted himself fortunate that he had lived to achieve it. It was the same with cattle and he thought himself blessed with a man like Willie Bartok to look after them, a man whose work and knowledge of the breeds made his path easier.

Doctor Leiper had an instinct for having men like Willie Bartok about him. He was a shrewd judge of character and for two years after coming to the Monkshood farm he had waited an opportunity to engage Willie Bartok, watching his work on a neighbouring farm with patient admiration. When the time came he fee-ed Willie long before the roup at the place he was leaving, before anybody else had the chance, tempting the man with a wage he could hardly refuse without being downright bad mannered. It was enough to give a man conceit of himself, but Willie Bartok was not that sort, and his only concern was to make sure the doctor never regretted engaging him. Oh aye, Willie had his suspicions about the doctor and his housekeeper, a fine carry on they were having the two of them if all was known, but it was none of Willie's business and he wasn't going to concern himself; the doctor was a good master and that was all that mattered to

Willie Bartok, except maybe when he had a drink with his cronies on a Saturday night at the Emporium, when Willie whiles said things about the ongoings at the Monkshood he didn't intend letting on about.

Meanwhile the shearing was in hand and the doctor had a word with Willie on how the work was progressing. A good clip Willie told him and the weight of wool would be well above average. Given an early start tomorrow he expected the shearers would be finished by dinner time. Today the sun burned from the heat hazed sky like a brick furnace, with not a breath of wind to blow away the flies, now lively over the sheep pens, tormenting man and beast in the heat of labour. Willie added that they would maybe have to dip the sheep again soon against fly-strike, the lambs at least before weaning.

On the last day of the shearing Willie Bartok had his brose as usual and the morning promised well for the clippers, with very little dew on the grass and the sky not too bright at this early hour. Willie lit his pipe when he left his cottage and walked down to the farm to fetch the dog for the gathering, the last field for the season, and glad he would be when it was over, though the trauchle of hay and peat moss still awaited them. It was sore on his feet with all the walking, though he wouldn't have to go round his sheep so often after they were clipped, as there would be less danger of the ewes dying on their backs once the wool was off. He could reduce his rounds to the normal twice a day instead of three or four times before the clipping, when the ewes were heavy in wool.

Willie got the dog out of his kennel and slipped his leash, the dog leaping ahead of him through the stackyard, where some of last year's corn stacks were still standing, to be threshed by portable mill later in the summer. Willie heard the dog barking between the ricks, which was most unusual for Rover 'cause he seldom barked. He must have come upon a weasel or a hedgehog to disturb him so, or maybe a rat in the ruck foons. Willie followed the barking around the flat circles of loose stones that were the foundations for stack building when he tripped on something that nearly knocked him over in his stride. It was the feet of a man in grey trouser legs, and as he followed the line of the suit to the body and the face he could hardly believe his own eyesight.

122

There was young Kenneth lying there behind a rick with his mouth wide open and staring up at the morning sky. But there was no light in those eyes and they gave no sign of recognition. God knows how long he had been there but probably most of the night. He was expected home this very day, most likely with flying colours from the university, or so his father hoped and would be waiting for him. Willie kneeled beside the young man and felt his pulse, the dog wagging his tail furiously, squeaking out his recognition and licking the cheeks of his young master. But there was no life in the cold wrist, the arm as limp and heavy as a piece of lead piping. Beyond the outstretched hand a small bottle lay amongst the stones. It was empty and Willie read poison on the label, then replaced it where it was lying. Willie had a twinge of conscience but he couldn't resist having a look at the envelope sticking out of the young man's breast pocket. It was an IOU gambling debt of nearly £300, something his father would have to meet, and Willie slipped it back where he found it, besides a photograph of his girl friend that had fallen out with the envelope.

Willie was trembling when he stood up, for he had gotten a bit of a fright, but he gathered his wits about him and walked back to the farmhouse. He rapped on the housekeeper's window but got no answer. So he took a long binder whip from the gig shed and tapped on his master's window upstairs. It was the housekeeper who opened the sash and looked down sullenly at the grieve. 'What is it Willie?' she asked, little above a whisper, not to waken the doctor; 'so early in the morning – you'd think it was lambing time, never mind the shearing.'

'Would you come down Miss Biper,' Willie said quietly, just loud enough for her to hear, 'I've got something to tell you, quiet like, before the doctor hears it.'

Inwardly Willie was thankful she had answered his tapping. He didn't want to be the one to break the news of such a tragedy to the old man. By telling the housekeeper she would relieve him of the ordeal.

'I'll be down Willie,' she called softly, then pulled down the window and closed the curtain.

But she was sleeping with the doctor. There could be no denying it now. Willie had seen for himself and he was convinced.

And those little bones he had dug up in the front garden – they were human after all. He had been sure of it but was afraid to mention it to anyone except his wife, least of all the housekeeper because of his suspicions. Now he was glad he hadn't. When Miss Biper fell with children the doctor would know how to get rid of them. Willie remembered those old days now and then when the housekeeper was indisposed, apparently with the influenza, and Bella was mistress in her absence. When Miss Biper recovered she would bury the evidence in the garden in the dead of night, deeper down than Willie was supposed to dig in his ordinary duties. Two or three nests of small bones he had dug up over the years and as quickly buried them again, afraid of what he had found. Willie knew fine it wasn't something the dog had buried. A pair of bloody butchers they were but you'd think they were saints. But with this new tragedy upon them he wouldn't tell a soul, except his wife, and maybe it would bring the pair of them to their senses.

And next time at the Emporium over his glass of beer Willie would tell his cronies that the doctor was a proper bloody gentleman, and he wouldn't be lying at that!

Two Men and a Boat

'The mere fact o' bein' alive wad kill ye come time!' Old Forbie Tait, farmer of Kingask, said this from time to time when some neighbour body died; whether he attended the funeral or no it was his stock phrase for the occasion, even though he knew fine that old Doolie Nash had drunk himself into his coffin, or that Waldie Podd had slaved himself to death for siller on that bit croft on the Windyhills above the kirk at Peatriggs, atween Slypigo there and Badengour. High on the face of the brae stood the kirk of Peatriggs, its bare stone spire polished by the wind and rain from the sea, a braw kirk and a fine monument to the devotion and industry of its congregation in the upkeep of such a place: an everlasting memorial to the indomitable spirit of man, far outlasting his brief span to grasp and spend, to lust and love, striving for a bite of meat and drink to keep him alive, with a vague promise of something better beyond the grave; something he didn't understand – clinging to a blind faith and a soulless purpose, nailed to the cross of life with no escape but death, and gathered at last to the cluster of gravestones that surrounded the kirk on the brae.

Always in your lug at Kingask was the growl and boom of the sea, swooshing over the rocks and boulders embedded on the beach; sometimes sullen and angry, tearing the seaweed from its roots and strewing it on the shore to the very edge of the road, where it rotted and stank in the summer sun and bred flies by the million. The next storm would submerge the dykes of rotting seaweed and reclaim it for the sea, the tang of fresh dulse strong in the wind, the undercurrent convulsing the water into monstrous waves, now careering ashore with their white manes rolling inwards, curving towards the beach, the white spume exploding over the rocks, drenching the road in lashings of spray. Next day, with a fall in the wind the sea would be quiet and peaceful,

125

caressing the shore in gentle playfulness, all bubbles and sunshine, blown froth and flotsam, lapping the roadside at high tide.

Outby Brochan was the lum of the gut factory, pointing out of the sea beyond the bents like a sore thumb, tall and gaunt and blackened with soot, the smoke curling out to sea in the herring season, or spreading over the land in a blue transparent haze, the smell of herring brine strong in the curing yards, your thoughts all pickle and trodden salt, like snow that had lain too long in a foul winter, giving a deeper boom to the growling of the sea, like a far off symphony on the waters.

When you left Brochan on the coast road to Candlebay, out by the gut factory, you could see the farmhouse at Kingask, like a beleaguered castle, with peep-hole dormers on the ark-shaped roof, loophole windows on its steep harled walls, with small stubby chimneys crowded on its gables. If you was looking for a fee out by on the Candlebay road the sight of this forbidding structure would have given you the shivers for a start, especially on a cold spring evening and the wind blowing through a harp of spray from the sea and the spindrift lashing the road. Kingask House stood apart from the village, just beyond the meal hill, like a fortress of formidable strength, the steep roof covered in the small slates of a former century, surrounded by a curtain wall enclosing the gardens, its pigeon-hole windows peering out like searching eyes over the green parks, the front door studded and hinged like the clasps on a sealed bible, with a boar's head knocker of wrought iron high up from the bare stone step and the rusting grill over the cellar.

Nor were you ever likely to forget that coast road the first spring evening you clapped eyes on the grey fortress farm of Kingask, the sky all ragged and torn by the north-east wind whipping off the sea, the fitful shafts of sunlight glancing on the water, the giant waves careering ashore, their white beards crested in foam, cascading against the rocks in fountains of flying spume, spilling out in bubbles and blown froth on the road, littering the beach with rich smelling seaweed torn from the ocean bed.

About two miles out along the coast you could see the village of Candlebay, huddled on the bents like a painting on a wall, with net poles on the links and ship masts in the tiny harbour, the wind-chopped sea stretching to the grey horizon.

It looked as if the North Sea was heaving a lash at the stranded fishing drifters that littered the two-mile stretch of coast from Brochan to Candlebay and Spitullie. About a dozen wooden steam drifters had been abandoned here and cast ashore by their owners; stripped of all valuable material, so that only the hulls and decks remained, towed round from the breakers' yards in Brochan and cut loose to find their own graves on the rocks, lashed ashore by incoming tides, to die ignominiously by the roadside. The villagers picked their bones when the tide was out, carting off all that they could manage for firewood; hacking first at the pinewood decks, then the oak and ash of the hulls, sparing nothing that would burn in their iron-barred grates, though the wood was impregnated with thirty years of sea salt. A few of the villagers set themselves up as firewood merchants and stripped the boats professionally. With big hammers they drove out the iron spikes and nails that held the planking together, first the decks and then the hulls, prising the boards apart with crowbars, leaving only the ribs sticking up from the shingle, so that folks called it the Drifters' Graveyard, and as one old skeleton disappeared another hull was cast adrift on the tide.

Jock Webster was king of the timber wolves, beating all his rivals with a second-hand motor-lorry, driving the wood inland to the farmers and cottars, selling it by the load. You soon got to know him once you was fee-ed at Kingask, and the difference between deck planking and hull timbers, though he charged a higher price for the pinewood, saturated for years in tar preservative, like railway sleepers, first-class kindling in the morning to boil your kettle quickly for brose making, before you started work in the byres.

Nearing Candlebay you could see the fishermen's houses, solid little structures of stone and lime, roofed with slates or red pantiles, gable on to the sea and the road, maybe as a safeguard against the sea-spray that flew over the roofs in stormy weather. Some of them were harled and whitewashed, others with the stonework around the doors and windows painted in different colours; one house green, another blue, one brown or yellow, others black and red, a picturesque rivalry that was both quaint and cheerful and full of character. The 'room' end of every house boasted an aspidistra or a Lily of the Valley in a brass or porcelain pot on a fretwork or polished hall table in the window, shrouded in floor length curtains of heavy material that was the last word in respectability, and you could nearly be sure that the family bible and hymn book would be lying on a table in the centre of the room; on a round polished table with carved legs, covered with white silk embroidery as a sort of miniature tabernacle for the Lord's anointed.

The fear of the Lord was great upon the fishermen and their families; a fear of His wrath that held them secure in the narrow paths of righteousness; a fear of the Lord who moved upon the water, who could catch a waterspout in the cup of His hand, or harbour a boat to safety with the blow of His breath – He who tilted the mighty iceberg with His fingertip, who strove against Satan and evil continually, and gave everlasting life to the faithful; He whose word was like the sound of restless seas in stony places.

But there were some who had forsaken the Lord and the mission halls, and had succumbed to the demon drink, or the vice of gambling and betting on horses, and these were frowned upon by the respectable fraternity, while the Witnesses of Jehova sought to gather the wayward sheep back to the shelter of the fold. But money was scarce in the hungry 'thirties, and though drink was cheap it never produced the debauchery of more recent times, for in those days the harvest of the sea was as profitless as the harvest of the land; more so since the end of the herring boom between the wars.

The little motor yawls of the fishermen were hauled up on the pebbled beach, or tethered to the piers in Candlebay harbour, which had been built for bigger boats in the days of the herring bonanza, but now deserted save for the few motor boats that swung at the ropes from the outthrusting capstans on the pierhead. When the tide was out you could see the wives and daughters of the fishermen gathering bait on the dark green slippery rocks out by the harbour mouth, while the men painted their yawls and net-floats that looked like a balloon festival in rainbow colours floating in the sunshine, and all the time the splash and swoosh of the waves and the cry of seagull and the rich tang of the sea.

128

There was even a boat-building yard at Candlebay, busy on the new seine-netters that were replacing the old steam drifters lying on the beach with their ribs in the sand. The new boats were also of wood, somewhat smaller than the old herring boats, and were propelled by the new diesel engines that were replacing steam. These new wooden boats were shortly to prove a Godsend against the magnetic mines of Hitler's secret armoury, sweeping them from the water where ships of steel couldn't go near them.

But now you were in the village and heading up the brae to the meal-mill and the miller's dam, where you rounded the corner and got your first close-up of the great house of Kingask, dwarfing the steading behind it; surely built as a tower keep you thought, big for a farm house, and must have been there for more than two-hundred years, even before the Jacobite risings.

But old Forbie Tait was no Jacobite; he was far too cautious for that and never liked taking chances, and although he took a passing interest in Royalty it was a fair bet he would never have joined Prince Charlie and his rebels. He was the ca-canny Scot who never liked feeing a lad on his first interview, but merely sized you up, prying out all the particulars he could gather of your past experience, so that he could form some opinion of your character, and not having a telephone wherewith to get your qualifications from your last employer he was obliged to look at your references. In a day or two, when he had time to think it over he would write and let you know if you was getting the job, meanwhile interrogating any other cheils who looked in by in answer to his appeal in the paper for a reliable cattleman, offering them the same terms of wait and see -- while Forbie made his choice at leisure. But you told old Forbie you was having none of that palaver, because it was getting too near the Term and you wanted to know where you stood; if he wasn't going to give you the job right away you was going to look somewhere else. He looked a bit abashed at this but had another think, and as a special favour for the man who had recommended you in the first place, an old grieve who had once worked at Kingask -- because of this Forbie decided to ignore precedent and take the risk of engaging you that very night while you sat in his kitchen at Kingask. You would get a pound-a-week in cash, which was £52 for the year, paid monthly, at the rate of £4 at the end of each month and the balance at the Martinmass and Whitsun Terms. This was a reduction of £2 over the year from what you was getting in your present employment as a dairy cattleman. But coming to beef cattle Forbie considered you would have an easier job and a Sunday off once a fortnight in winter (when the foreman would look after your nowt – once you had sorted them in the morning) and you wouldn't have to get up so early in the mornings as you did in the dairy byres; five-thirty would be early enough to be ready to start at six, after you had your breakfast, two hours later than you was in dairy work. And you would get the usual perquisites: coal, meal, milk and tatties, house and garden, and you would be allowed to keep about a dozen hens, provided you wired them in so that they couldn't scratch in the fields. So it was all settled and you got a cup of tea from the mistress at Kingask, a pleasant enough like woman with common-sense talk, and then it was time for you to take the coast road again on your bike, past the drifters' graveyard, this time in the dark with your new electric dynamo, which was attached to the rim of your rear wheel, heading for Brochan and the Bogside.

So here was you fee-ed to go to Kingask, where you would get away from the skitter and chauve of the dairy byres, and you'd get a longer lie in the mornings and a Sunday off, which was something to crow about in those days of slavery. Wilberforce should have freed the slaves at home before he concerned himself with those in Africa and the southern states of America: the industrial workers, the miners and the farm servants; especially the farm workers, who in some instances had worse working and living conditions than the negroes he campaigned for. If ever there was a case for charity beginning at home this was it, where for several decades after Wilberforce, even to the end of the first quarter of the twentieth century, British farm workers were still working within sight of Uncle Tom's Cabin, and there were still quite a number of whip-cracking Simon Lagrees amongst our farming cheils – not all of them of course and some were gentlemen, but they were a minority.

But your new job with Forbie Tait gave you a feeling of confidence in those last few anxious weeks before the May Term, a period of grim uncertainty for the cottar, until the breadwinner had some prospect of a roof over his head and a bite for his family

in the coming year, and when this had been attained a new sense
of security and a feeling of renewed independence soon began to
show. Now you could snap your fingers at folk who thought they
had you in a corner – not having a house or a job (or so they
thought, because you kept those things to yourself for a while)
cowering under their authority, while all the time you was laughing up your sleeve, and now you could tell them to go to hell
because you was going to Kingask. Trouble was that the same
thing would likely happen again in a couple of years, when you'd
be cursing Forbie Tait; but meantime you blessed him for what
you thought was a new freedom, a new lease of life – and so it
went on in the cottar's lot.

Forbie sent a motor lorry to flit you, not that you had much in
the way of furniture, but a few bits of sticks and dishes and bedding and a crate of hens. In fact your kitchen dresser had cost
you only four shillings and sixpence at a second-hand sale and
was little better than a hen coop. But there you was with all you
possessed in the world and you bundled Kathleen and the bairn
into the lorry cab beside the driver and his second man and sat
on the load yourself, clinging to the ropes while the cold wind
whistled about your ears. The only thing you remembered about
that flitting was the speed of the lorry, like you thought they'd
have all your dishes broken and your furniture out of joint,
tearing on like that, just to have their Saturday afternoon off,
which was something you didn't get on the farms; like you was
just cottar dirt and it didn't matter much for the bits of stick you
had for furniture, so long as Forbie Tait paid for the flitting, and
you felt like telling the driver this, for you was fell annoyed when
you got off the load at the cottar houses at Kingask, high up on
the hill above the sea and the parks.

Here then was the second cottar house Kathleen and you had
flitted to, the first one with a young bairn between you. It was a
double cottar house, with the chimneys from both sections on the
middle of the slated roof, and stone porches at the gables. Badgie
Summers that was foreman lived in the nearest half-house and
you would have the end biggin' furthest from the road. The porch
was handy for a pram or a bicycle or such like; besides the pails
of water you would have to carry up the brae from the tap at the
farm. The back bedroom window looked down on the village and

the sea, now deep blue and spume flecked in the face of a stiff breeze coming off the land. Badgie Summers was home for his dinner and he gave you a carry inside with your furniture, no doubt casting a critical eye over your bits and pieces, thinking it was hard times for young folk setting up house, for no doubt being an older man he would have better furniture; the older, heavier stuff of solid mahogany, substantial compared with the flimsy material you was getting nowadays, and soon riddled with woodworm. But you had your bed, table, chairs and dresser; dressing-table with mirror (with two paintings by Constable on the sidewings) washstand, meal-girnal and your chaumer kist, about all you could afford in those hungry times, second-hand at that, besides your bedding and curtains, pots and pans and dishes. The only odd bit of furniture in your load was a glass case with a model ship in it, a cardboard cut-out of a steam cargo boat you had made in the evenings of your spare time; an unusual hobby for a farm Jock, and while Badgie carried it into the house he remarked that you had fairly come to the right place for makin' boats, and you supposed that he meant the boat building yard down in the village. Of course you was just fair daft on boats at this time of your life and your daftness was expressed in your efforts with models, though you had no real desire to go to sea in any practical sense.

But it was good of Badgie to give you some assistance with your furniture, the first time you had seen the man: round faced, high coloured and beardless, not even a moustache, with keen blue eyes that shone like polished gig lamps, his cap on a slant on his short cropped head, bull-necked with massive shoulders, wearing his kersey-tweed trousers and dark blue fisherman's ganzie, like the men wore in the village (but without the smell of herring about him) and you would have thought to look at him that he was a sort of crofter-fisherman who didn't know much about the bigger farms you had been accustomed to and their ways of working away inland from the coast, though he spoke in the doric tongue as broad as you'd hear many miles inland from the sea. His wife took Kathleen and the bairn inside until you had the furniture unloaded, then treated the pair of you to a bite of dinner and a cup of tea, real neighbourly folk, and then Kathleen put the bairn in the pram and Badgie's youngest quine diddled him about for most of the afternoon, while Kathleen helped you to lay the bit linoleum you had kept from the last place for your bedroom floor and gave you a hand to set up the bed. She then hung curtains on the windows, with white lace screens nearest the glass and placed her pot flowers on the sills. You left her to scrub the cement floor in the kitchen while you tidied up your odds and ends in the garden shed and fastened your hens into the ree.

Badgie Summers was a big hardy cheil who had survived the Kaiser's War and he called his medals 'badges', the medals he had won for his dour courage on the Western Front and he sometimes wore them on Remembrance Day at the kirk, so the folk just called him 'Badgie'. After the war he had married and cottared at Langstraik, one of Forbie's out-farms, but for the last twelve years he had worked full-time at Kingask. He worked three horses instead of the usual pair, 'cause Forbie Tait liked to have a spare horse resting in the stable, taking it in turns as a pair at the plough or harrows, mower or tattie-digger, and the only time he had the three yoked as a team was for the five-tyned grubber in spring or for the binder in hairst. Forbie had a great care for his horse beasts and never liked to see them tagged with wark or besotted in rain, their fetlocks matted in frosted mud and needing a wash with soft soap. Forbie never liked that, nor did he puddle his folk either, and if you was pulling wet turnips on the brae above the steading, or ploughing lea by the shore, at the first patter of rain Forbie or his son Tom would whistle you home, so you had no need of an oilskin suit and it was your own fault if you got wet through. The lad that was foreman before Badgie didn't always listen to Forbie's whistle, or pretended not to hear it and kept on ploughing in the rain, maybe because he didn't like cleaning harness or mixing hen feed up in the loft, which was the sort of job Forbie would have waiting for him under a roof. When he lowsed at last in a heavy downpour and came home with his pair Forbie was waiting for him in the stable. The lad was taking off the harness from the wet backs of his mares and hanging it on the pegs, his own jacket as wet as them, when Forbie says to him: 'By gum lad,' says he, 'ye can tak' a spaad and gyang ootside an' de'l neuks if ye like but ye're nae gaun tae puddle my

133

horse!' But after sixteen years in Forbie's service Badgie knew the old man better than this and always lowsed his horse when the rain came on.

The beasts always came first on most farms. It was for the sake of the horses that you got two hours for your dinner; not so that the horseman could rest, for half the time he was supposed to be grooming and feeding them, and the two hours gave them plenty of time to chew and masticate their hay, though they never lay down in the stall at dinner time. It was the same with cattle: a stirk in a stall was always more important than the man who fed him; worth more commercially than a stockman who could be had for £1 a week in the glutted labour markets, while a nowt beast would be worth £20 to £25 once he was fattened for the butcher. But Forbie usually put human being before beast, which couldn't be said of most farmers in the days between the wars.

One of the pleasantries of your early days at Kingask was wakening up around six-o'clock on a Sunday morning in summer, getting up and going over to the bedroom window to see the foreman taking your three cows from pasture into the wee byre for milking. This happened once a fortnight in summer, on your Sunday off, a fine change from the dairy byre, where such indulgence was unheard of; when you had to be there yourself every morning, Sunday or week-day, at 4am sharp, unless you were ill or had taken a moonlit flit, for sleepin' in wasn't allowed for and was liable to bring you the sack.

But here at Kingask you had a beef cattle herd that required no attention while on summer grazing, and with only three milk cows in your charge, milked by the kitchiedeem, you had much less responsibility. On the Sunday mornings that Badgie took in the kye he stood in the byre and smoked his pipe, leaning over a travis post while the lassie filled her pails from the warm bulging udders. When it was your Sunday on duty you milked the cows yourself, and the kitchie lassie got her full Sunday off, a relief service which had been performed previously by Edith, Forbie's younger daughter, until the women folk discovered that you was a practised hand milker, then wouldn't give you peace or you did it. Badgie couldn't milk and had no desire to learn (especially when he was a horseman) nor was he keen that you should do it either, because when it happened on week days it sometimes kept you from the field work, which didn't please Badgie if he thought he was getting too much to do on his own. Indeed there were surprisingly few menfolk who could milk a cow by hand, the good old-fashioned way, thinking maybe it was a bit below their dignity, especially if they were horsemen, and so they left it to the women, never realizing the finger cramping exercise it really was. But being a dairy cattleman you had learned this excruciating art, though in this case you got nothing extra from old Forbie for your pains; nothing beyond the knowledge that you was giving his daughter a longer lie in bed on Sunday mornings, besides the satisfaction that you was giving the homesick kitchie-deemie a longer day at home with her family; indeed her sweet smile of thankfulness made it seem worth your while.

On most of the beef farms it was also your duty to take a stroll through the pastures on Sunday mornings to check on the cattle: stots, heifers, stirks or yearlings, breeding cows and calves, counting their numbers in each park, to make sure none were ill, strayed or stolen, an exercise which might have taken you just over an hour, provided there wasn't water to be pumped somewhere to their watering troughs, which took a while longer of your time. But old Forbie liked to go through the cattle fields himself on Sundays (as he did on week days) maybe as a mode of exercise, but he wouldn't pump the water. So you looked from your other window at the front of the house (your kitchen window) and there was Forbie in his parks, clad in his usual brown suit and checked cap, pipe in mouth, the reek flying over his shoulder, one hand behind his back, the other waving his walking stick, slashing at the odd thistle or tanzy you had missed with your scythe.

Ah well, on Sunday mornings such as these, when you looked from your bedroom window and saw Badgie Summers taking in your kye – somebody else doing your work – you just smiled to yourself and crept back into bed with Kathleen, warm and cosy (provided the bairn wasn't standing up in his crib howling for his milk bottle) and you'd fair think you was King of the Castle. It was usually oatbread and cheese for breakfast, because Kathleen was an excellent baker of oatcakes, and as oatmeal was a perquisite it paid you to have a wife who could bake; especially if

135

you could buy a kebbock of home-made cheese from the farm wife, or from one of the crofters, and with good strong tea to wash it down, with cream and sugar, and then some scones and mar-malade – well, there wasn't much to complain about. And then you could light your pipe and sit down in your second-hand armchair and get stuck into the Film Weekly or the Picturegoer you had bought on the Saturday night when you was at the pictures in Brochan. Kathleen would be spoon-feeding the bairn on her knee at the table, a bib under his chin, while he mumbled some sort of mumbo-jumbo between the spoonfuls, kicking his mother's legs and reaching for anything on the table he could get his hands on, and sometimes toppling the sugar bowl.

But you was far away in Hollywood, reading all the gossip about the film stars: their marriages and divorces, their next starring roles, like Robert Donat in *The Ghost Goes West*, Shirley Temple in *Curly Top*, or Katherine Hepburn in *Mary of Scotland*, and there were whispers of a young crooner called Frank Sinatra. Then you read the film reviews, production news, etc., admiring all the exotic stills and bathing beauties, which would absorb you till nearly dinner time, and you could still jump on your bike and get the Sunday papers if you wished, 'cause you was a glutton for newsprint. After dinner you could hoe the tatties you had planted in the garden, now well above the ground, or weed your vegetables, then rig yourself in your marriage suit (the only one you possessed) and when Kathleen got dressed the pair of you would take the bairn in the pram to the village, round the closed shops and the deserted harbour, and two or three times you'd gone right into Brochan, on to the beach and the promenade, where you each had an ice-cream cone from the vendors, sometimes two, because the Italians in Brochan had awfully good ice-cream, and you'd give the bairn a lick at your cones in the by-going, smiling up at you there so pleased like, despite the cold sea wind that whipped at the pram hood, even in the height of summer, for it was always cold in Brochan.

On the way back you'd wheel the pram up Mid Street, so that you could see the stills at the Picture House, black and white and glossy, and the hand-bills with all the particulars of next week's programmes, so that you could make a choice of at least one night's showing, though most likely you'd go yourself and Kathleen would have to stay at home with the bairn, unless it was a special programme you wanted her to see – pictures like *Mutiny on the Bounty*, with Clark Gable and Charles Laughton, *Under Two Flags*, with Ronald Colman and Claudette Colbert, *How Green Was My Valley*, or *Back Street*, pictures with a romantic or feminine appeal you knew Kathleen would enjoy, for she was no addict of the cinema and you had to select her films. With you it was different and most of the run-of-the-mill pictures appealed to your infatuated imagination, and that to such an extent that you was almost incapable of criticism, a worshipper who could find no fault in his gods, or should you say goddesses, for it was the great days of Garbo, or Dietrich, or Barbara Stanwyck and Irene Dunn, those whose every gesture, every smile, every tear was watched and dreamed upon and cried over by millions in those days.

On such occasions when Kathleen accompanied you to the cinema Mrs Summers next door took in the bairn, little Brian. It didn't happen often but when it did Mrs Summers was delighted. She liked bairns, and so did her daughters, especially Esma, the one still at school, and between them they spoiled the brat, even to such an extent that he would hardly claim his mother when she came back, so that Esma had to come round with him in her arms and lay him in his crib before he was content. As it was he sometimes crawled along to the Summers' doorstep, and later, when he got on his feet he ran round half-naked (when his mother had removed his pants for toilet) and when he saw Badgie and yourself coming up the road for dinner, he would come running down the road to meet you, running right between the pair of you with his bare bum, even on the coldest days, and Badgie would say: 'Man, that's the wye I like tae see a bairn brocht up; nae need o' yer coddelt bairns but hardy as they come!'

Then there was the time that Kathleen went down the close for water, and Mrs Summers and Esma saw her go past the window, and once she was well down the brae, Esma ran round and took little Brian out of his crib, still with his dumb-teat in his mouth, where Kathleen thought he would be safe or she returned, and Esma ran round with him in her arms and hid herself in her mother's bedroom. Kathleen had been gone about ten minutes, and the first thing she did on her return was to look in the crib,

137

and when the bairn wasn't there she went in a state, wondering where he could be. She looked over all the house, even up the stairs, thinking she knew not what but nowhere could she find him; so she ran round to Mrs Summers and gasped out that the bairn had disappeared.

'Disappeared!' cried Mrs Summers, pretending shocked surprise.

'Aye,' said Kathleen, 'I went to the waal for watter and left him in his crib. When I cam' back he wasna there and I've searched high and low for him!'

'Gweedsake,' said Mrs Summers, 'but he canna be far awa'. Did ye leave the side o' the crib doon?'

'No,' said Kathleen, 'I left it up, so that he couldna get oot; he could never climb owre the top o' his crib. I juist canna think whaur he can be.'

Kathleen was beginning to get hysterical and Mrs Summers could hardly keep in her laugh, while all the time pretending to be serious.

But even with jam on the dumb-teat Esma couldn't keep the bairn quiet any longer in the back room, and he gave himself away with one of his little gurgles.

Esma emerged from the bedroom with the bairn in her arms and Kathleen took him from her a little angrily, for she had been on the verge of tears in her anxiety.

But it was soon forgotten and after school hours Esma would jab the back of their fireplace with the poker, and when Kathleen heard the dunts in the back of her grate she knew it was a signal to come round, mostly to play cards for an hour before she made the supper, with little Brian at her knee.

Another time Esma knocked in the evening, which wasn't usual for her; just before the lamp was lit and you could scarcely read the papers, and when Kathleen ran round Badgie was sitting reading the daily paper with a stump of candle burning on his head.

'See what the bitches have come till,' he cried to Kathleen, 'they wunna licht the bludy lamp tae lat me see tae read the papers.'

But after a month or two with Badgie Summers you soon learned that he knew a lot more about farming than his fisherman's jersey gave him credit for, especially at hoeing time when he could spot a charlock weed among the turnip plants before you could see it; particularly among the yellow turnips, which it most closely resembles, more so than swedes, because of its coarse leaf and lighter colouring, and with your untrained eye you would have singled out the charlock and left it for a healthy yellow turnip at the end of your hoe-blade, a useless weed that sprouted a yellow flower and podded seed but never grew a bulb to feed hungry cattle. This coastal strip of Pittentumb abounded in the yellow charlock weed, known all over the Bogside as the skelloch, and the folks near the coast blamed their ancestors for bringing it on to the land with the seaweed, carting up the dykes of rotted dulse and tangleweed from the shores, using it on their crofts as fertilizer. Of course a body had no real proof of this; maybe it was that the richness of the dulse, impregnated with iron and iodine, encouraged the charlock to grow more profusely round the North Sea coast, where the grain and turnip fields were sometimes as yellow as though you had sown them with mustard seed, while on the inland farms of the Bogside the yellow menace was much less prevalent. It is an oily seed that grows only on the blackened furrow and is never seen on healthy grass, lying dormant in the under soil for a decade; perhaps for ever, but bursting into flower wherever the plough has broken the surface to give it air and life.

Coming from an inland fairm toon a body was much less accustomed to the charlock plant, especially in its younger stages in the turnip drills, when the leaves are the size of a 'moosie's lug', as they say in the Bogside, which is a good size for starting the hoe. Badgie had been brought up with the weed; well aware of its disguise in the seedling turnip drills. No wonder then at the end of your first hoeing season at Kingask that Badgie took you (literally by the lug) to the turnip park and pointed out your yellow drill alternately with his own that didn't have a yellow flower to be seen in them. All over the park every second drill blossomed its yellow flower; for now, about six weeks after hoeing, the charlock was in bloom, which of course it isn't at hoeing time, being then but an inconspicuous seedling of the 'moosie's lug' variety, but no damned use to anybody. Nor could you deny your incompetence, because there were only the two of you at the hoe, with nobody else to blame, so it was easy to pick out your yellow drill, beginning second from the dyke. No wonder that old Forbie himself had paid you a visit at the hoe (for maybe Badgie had been watching your drill from the corner of his eye and reported it – not caring to mention it himself) and Forbie had bent down and pulled out a charlock seedling you had left and asked if you knew what that was? Maybe they'd had this experience before with strangers. But of course you were so cocksure of yourself in those days you said 'Aye,' that it was a skelloch; that you knew fine what it was, thinking they were taking the raise of you, while all the time they were merely biding their time to confirm their suspicions that you didn't know, or at least that your eye wasn't yet properly trained to spot the charlock weed in such profusion with the yellow turnip seedlings. In the maincrop swedes however you were more or less faultless; with a clean, well-dressed drill, and perhaps for this they overlooked your other failings.

All the same you had enjoyed hoeing that season with Badgie Summers, just the two of you in a fifteen acre field, up on the brae above the farm and the cottar houses, cold and windswept in winter but warm and sunny enough in the long days of summer. Badgie had a great hairst of war stories and a firm belief in the Tory Government, headed at that time by Stanley Baldwin, and later by Neville Chamberlain as Prime Minister. Of course you never adhered to any political party and simply declared yourself Independent, so that you had no political arguments with Badgie. If you had been a staunch Labour man, or even a Liberal, you would have been the odd man out in any case, because most of the farmers were Tories and they drove their workers to the polls in their own cars, throwing hints that they should vote Conservative, seeing they were getting a hurl, and this was the myth that kept Sir Robert Boothby so long in Parliament as their representative at Westminster. But sitting on the fence as an Independent they couldn't make head nor tail of you, and you escaped a lot of useless argument.

But you listened to Badgie's wartime exploits with great relish, especially about the huge skirling shells that the Germans sent over the Scottish trenches. The Scots called them 'coalboxes', because of their great size and black smoke in explosion, and they seemed to make a noise like 'Faur-ee-bidin'? Faur-ee-bidin'? Faur-ee-bidin'?' which, translated from the doric simply means 'Where are you staying?' repeated several times very quickly as the shell hurtled overhead, searching out the kilted Scots, then made some attempt to answer its own question by crumping down with a tremendous explosion in some Scottish trench or supply line behind the front. Badgie took the mick out of the British army 'Bull' and spit-and-polish mania that existed during the First World War. He said the Germans were untidy in comparison and didn't have to wash and shave all the time; some of them even had beards, and though the British Tommies were allowed a moustache (neatly trimmed) they went about most of the time like scraped pigs. Badgie told the story of the sergeant in the Gordon Highlanders who was daft on discipline and square bashing: how he gave the order 'Stack rifles,' then formed his platoon in a straight line the whole length of the barrack square, dressing from the right, and marched them to within a few inches of the stone wall. 'Halt!' he cried. 'Eyes front,' then 'At ease . . . sporrans aside . . . up kilts . . . down pants . . . out cocks . . . and . . . wait for it . . . wait for it . . . and . . . PISH!'

There was also the story of the Scottie home on leave, a postie from Candlebay, and when someone remarked to him that the Somme had been a terrible battle he replied: 'Och aye man, the human heids were comin' stottin' doon the hill like neeps and buggerin' a' the wye!' 'I stood whaur thoosins fell,' said another, trying to go one better, though it wasn't a thing to brag about, nor to be laughed at. 'Aye Sandy,' said a cronie, who knew 'Sandy' as a bit of a braggart, 'it had been whan ye changed yer sark ah doot!' Then there was the case of the discharged Highlander who married a dubious lady of the streets and on their bridal night she removed her wig, her glass eye, and then her false teeth, each time remarking: 'How do ye like to be done Jock?' By this time Jock was undressed so he pulled up his nightgown and cried: 'Shot off at Mons woman – foo div YE like tae be done?'

You had met only a very few of these men on the farms in your own lifetime who could fully grasp and discuss world politics with intelligence and Badgie was one of them. Some of them (excluding the war veterans) were almost totally unaware of the world and its ways beyond the parish boundaries, though they knew these boundaries extremely well, and most of the folks within them; all their faults and foibles, their varied characters and chitter-chatter, and whose intimate affairs occupied their ultimate perimeter of thought. The better informed on a wider scale were those who read their employer's newspapers, mostly one with a conservative slant, though that didn't matter; it was the information that was important, before the days when radio became popular on the farms – when you heard it only in the chip-shops or in the pubs when you went into the towns. Most of the cottars had gramophones, but these were for entertainment, not for political reform, but for 'Cornkisters' and Hilly Billy singers of 'Old Faithful' and 'Home on the Range', or any song or instrumental item that was popular at the time, like Gene Autry with his guitar, George Formby with his ukelele, or Gracie Fields singing like a lintie.

But though Badgie was well informed from his master's newspaper he was by no means educated or cultured: it was merely a village pump, pub-crawl knowledge that he had of the world and it suited his purpose, and once he had filled and lighted his pipe at the end of a long and weary turnip drill you could enjoy his lively talk on world affairs right to the other end, forgetting your twisted neck and aching shoulder muscles in Badgie's rapporteur; in fact he lightened the work and shortened the time and the drills with his well-informed newsing. And Badgie wasn't a bore or a blabber-mouth and he was easy to listen to; and a good listener too when it was your turn. And there was plenty to talk about in the middle of the 'Hungry Thirties', or during the two years you was at Kingask: what with Mussolini's rape of the Abyssinians; General Franco and the Spanish Civil War; Japanese aggression in Manchuria; Hitler's expansion in Europe; the death of King George V; the abdication of Edward VIII, and the unsettled state of the monarchy at home – no end of subjects for discussion, and Badgie had a good smattering of knowledge and a strong opinion on most of them. In fact it could be added that Badgie's involvement in world politics was partly to blame for your detachment from removing the charlock weeds from the turnips plants; in that he was taking your mind off your work, but blissfully so.

And while the grey sea growled endlessly on the coast, and

142

the cloud patterns changed in the sky, Badgie had his say, while you listened intently and drew on your pipe subconsciously. He told you how he was come of cottar folk, and that his father had been a grieve for most of his working life on the bigger farms further up the coast. His father had died of a festered throat he said, swallowing the poisonous pus in his sleep when the boil had burst, almost choking him when he awoke, and that the poison went all through his body and killed him, leaving his wife with a growing, school-age family, and nothing but parish relief to support them. All caused by working on the farms in the rain Badgie said, and catching a chill from his wet clothes. Badgie now had a wife and son and two fine daughters; the son married and cottared somewhere, the oldest quine fee-ed at a fairm toon, while Esma the youngest quine was still at the school in the village. His wife was a stoutish well-faced woman with a friendly smile and disposition, and as things turned out almost a mother to your Kathleen when your own little Winifred was born.

Forbie Tait himsel' was a rigorous master, though not a hard one, but set in his ways and thrawn to change; eccentric almost in his conservative attitude to life and farming, and fortunate that he had lived a decade before the catastrophic upheaval of the second agricultural revolution. He was the lessee with the oldest tenancy on the estate; indeed he was born on it, though on a different farm, up at Langstraik there, which was farmed nowadays by his oldest son, Maxwell Tait. Forbie's long tenancy of Kingask was honoured by the Laird of Slypigo on reaching its fiftieth anniversary, when he and his family were entertained to a grand dinner and wine-out in the big hoose up at Boganchero, attended by all the swanks, lawyers, factors and contractors, and all the other tenant farmers on the estate and their wives and families, when Forbie was presented with the Laird's crest and insignia, with his own name engraved on it and the number of years he had faithfully paid his rent (though that wasn't mentioned) but it gave account of his long years of good husbandry on the farms of Kingask and Langstraik, though for his work on Kingask in particular. So you could say that Forbie Tait lived in a tied house, just like his cottars, under the jurisdiction of his Laird, in the same way as you was responsible to Forbie; the only real difference being that you paid a sub-let rent to Forbie with your labour, while he paid the Laird in cash, and any major neglect on Forbie's part was likely to land him out on the road with his flitting, all of which when you thought about it made the great tower house of Kingask seem less impressive or desirable.

Kingask lay on the north side of the Mattock Hill, though you couldn't see it from the farmhouse, only from the top of the brae above the cottar houses; a shapeless hillock hardly worthy of notice, grey and featureless in sun or shadow, the sky above it sometimes mitred into a dome of hammered lead, or the wispy clouds all corrugated and torn apart in the struggle between wind and rain in the elements of weather change; the hill shrouded in mist above the green parks that stretched all the way from above Peatriggs to Slypigo, over the Windyhills from Badengour, where the sea raged in a fury against the cliff face.

What with your literary turn of mind and your flair for the movies it could be said that at this stage o° your life you imagined yourself as a sort of country bred Charles Dickens; just as in a later time in your rustic existence you associated yourself with Mark Twain, after you had seen his filmed biography, all of which may be a form of mild insanity, but also a source of inspiration which most artists experience in their desire to emulate their betters (hero-worship if you like) reaching for the star that shines at the top of the ladder they are scaling. In the present instance you had just seen David O. Selznick's version of *David Copperfield*, and you was reading a copy of *A Tale of Two Cities*, so the influence of the great novelist was strong upon you. But there was a cosiness in Selznick's production of the famous classic that you couldn't match in your spartan existence as a poor cottar in one of the most remote corners of our country's coastline; not even in pastoral style, because of the bleakness of the landscape and the withering climate. But in Kathleen at least you had all the beauty and warmth and sweetness of Maureen O'Sullivan, Selznick's choice of heroine, and in Kathleen also you had a competent cook and mother and housewife, far superior in health and spirit to the delicate, fragile, frivolous Dora, devoted to her wayward pomeranian poodle – and though Kathleen was fond of cats she would never fuss over them as Dora did or put them before her husband. Such was the conceit of your literary mind

144

at the moment and the novel that was in you would have a long time to wait.

When the winter came on you was obliged to Badgie to supper your nowt in the evenings when you went to the pictures in Brochan, about once a week; feeding the cattle in the byres with fresh hay and shaking up their bedding with a fork, a service that old Forbie insisted upon, and had bargained for with you at feeing time. Badgie did the job when he suppered his horses, when Forbie and young Tom would be in the stable with him for a blether, taking the neighbours through hand or any political tittle-tattle that had been in the papers, like Baldwin's decision not to let King Edward VIII marry Mrs Simpson; or Hitler's march into Czechoslovakia, things like that, which did interest you to a certain extent, but not to the length of one whole hour and thirty minutes, which was the common length of their stable sessions, evening after evening, every night of the week, while you stood there with your flagon of milk, bored to silence on your wearied feet (after a hard day's work) because nobody sat on the cornkist, and you would have been considered lazy had you tried it. So you just stood there waiting patiently for the foreman to blow out the lantern and close the stable door, for to have left before him would have been considered the height of bad manners – even on the excuse that the bairn needed his milk before bedtime. Kathleen was wearied waiting for you and the bairn's milk, but when you whispered this to Badgie and said you would have to be home sooner he said you was henpecked and that he wouldn't put up with it, and that if it was the pub he was in he would stay as long as he liked and that no white-faced woman would stop him. Kathleen said he was a selfish brute for this and that you should come home sooner in spite of him, although of course you never did, in case you offended him, or that he thought you unmanly.

On your visits to the movies on winter evenings you escaped these stable gossip sessions, much obliged though you was to Badgie for attending to your cattle, especially as he seldom required you to do the same for him in the stable, supperin' his horse, because the only time he went out was on Saturday night, down to the pub in the village with the blacksmith, and the two of them looked in by the stable on their way back after closing time. When you was away at the movies Badgie brought your flagon of milk home with his own and left it on your doorstep, rapping on the window to let Kathleen know it was there, and that she could get her bairn fed, and on these occasions Kathleen said he was usually earlier than other evenings when you was with him. And maybe you got your character in the stable behind your back when you wasn't there to defend yourself.

But sometimes there was a cow calving, not only the milch cows but maybe one of the sucklers, there being about a dozen of them on the farm, and as you couldn't ask Badgie to watch these as well you had to look in at the byre yourself on your way back from watching Dorothy Lamour as *The Jungle Princess*, or Ginger Rogers in *Don't Bet on Love*, and if Polly-Wolly-Doodle was in labour, or Little Dolly Dander (for so you had them named) you had to take off the jacket of your marriage suit – the only one you had – put on an old waterproof and give such assistance as was necessary. On the night you saw *Rose Marie* Gorgonzola gave birth to a fine son. You called her this because of her mixed blue and white colouring, marbled like the famous cheese, a big-boned friendly animal, though most of the others were red shorthorns. So, with the Ave Marias of Jeanette Macdonald and Nelson Eddy still ringing in your ears you helped deliver Gorgonzola of a swarthy bullock, still with the chain about her neck, eager to lick him dry, so to please her you dragged him up beside her, and being a suckler she was allowed to mother him until his weaning. First thing in the morning you'd get a bucket of warm water from the farm kitchen, with a dash of oatmeal, and give it to Gorgonzola to drink, besides the first pailful of her own milk, after the calf had been fed, something that these old farmers insisted upon, and maybe that was why they had never heard of staggers or milk fever, because they were replacing a deficiency the natural way, or as they say – a gallon a day keeps the vet away.

The only time Badgie required your assistance was the night his roan mare gave birth to a foal, when you sat up all night with him in the loose box, where the mare had plenty of room to throw herself about, nickering to Badgie and staring at him when she felt the pains coming on. 'Hae patience lass,' Badgie would say. 'It's a lang time or mornin',' adding that she had herself to blame for taking up her time with that stallion in the springtime. Old Forbie had supplied you both with a bundle of Chamberi's Journals as reading material, where you lay on the straw under the lantern, and about midnight young Tom came out with a cup of tea and shortbread. The mare foaled suddenly about four o'clock in the morning, without much help from either of you, a furry like creature with a white spot on his forehead and legs like a giraffe, and after it was over Badgie said you'd better go home and get an hour's sleep before you started in the byre, that he would be in no hurry yoking up until well after breakfast when the foal would be footed and reaching for his mother's teats.

Having had considerable experience as a dairy cattleman you had some idea of how to produce milk from the three cows under your charge at Kingask. Not so much in summer of course when these things are governed by the weather and the state of the pasture; but during the winter months when the cows were hand fed you knew what to give them to encourage butter-fat in quantity as well as quality. It wasn't long or Deborah and Edith were expressing their surprise at the thickness of the overnight cream on the milk basins and on their porridge bowls, which would nearly float a penny they said; enabling them to churn more butter and curd more cheese than they had ever done before from three cows, even with a separator. Even Mistress Tait herself commended you on the new richness of their milk yield and wondered what you could be feeding those cows on to give such cream. Of course old Forbie must have known that you was rather heavy on the bran supply, and the kitchiedeem knew that you came to the scullery every evening at tea time for a pail of warm water, and with this you mixed a sloppy bran mash for three dairy cows, adding a little crushed oats (besides draff when you could get it) and they licked it out clean from the feed troughs, when you would throw in a handful of oilcake as bonus (which was meant for fattening cattle) and even though one of the cows was almost dry – which nearly always happens pending a calving – and there had to be calvings, the increased rations of the other two soon made good the deficiency.

But it wasn't only in milk production that you was gradually gaining favour with old Forbie Tait of Kingask, for in your first winter on the place you had actually produced fat cattle for the Christmas sales while still carrying their first teeth, a feat young Tom or even Forbie himself had never seen in his life before. Neither had you for that matter, and if they had asked you how you had managed it you couldn't have told them. But to them it was an achievement worthy of discussion at the stable meetings, especially on the evenings that you wasn't there to hear it (but away at the pictures) except that Badgie told you the next day. So it was at least a credit to your efficiency and diligence in attending to these beasts during the long months of early winter. Of course they were a good class of bullocks before you ever saw them; Aberdeen-Angus mostly, for Forbie bought only the best in the store-cattle rings, paying such a price for them he said that they left only their dung as profit (after paying wages) there being such a small margin to work on between the store and fat cattle prices. But Forbie slivered down his pipe when he said this and spat in the close; the bigger the lie the bigger mouthful so to speak, like it was when he told you he had been farming out of capital since the Liberals went out, though he still voted for the Tories. But he took these bullocks off the waning pasture in early autumn, in the middle of harvest really, inside to tares and green corn in the byres, which gave you the long end of the year to finish them off with hay and early turnips (or what had been left of them after your dastardly hoeing), crushed corn and oil-cake, ready for the Christmas sales.

All the same Forbie was delighted with your efforts in the byres, and although he didn't give you anything extra for your pains he rang your praises loudly to the neighbour folk, and when they weren't there to listen there was always Badgie Summers. Badgie would be ploughing in the muck you had spread out on the stubble, well up on the brae, when Forbie would take an afternoon dander to see how he was doing, or maybe just to pass the time and get away for a while from the women folk, walking beside Badgie for a couple of rounds to stretch his legs, making good use of his staff, talking to his foreman, while Jug and Dandy strained at the yoke and swingletrees, snorting out their white breath in the mild frost that hung over the stubble fields, biting on the steel bits that held them so tightly to the reins in Badgie's hands; heads down, necks curved, plodding canny forwards, harness glinting in the weak sun over their backs, their tails tied up with tufts of straw, exposing the shorn rumps; their legs and bellies clipped bare to a straight line from breast to hind hip, Badgie walking behind the closing furrow, one foot in front of the other in the narrow trench, 'the ploughman's gait', as they called it, while he listened to his master and never slackened a step.

Now if there was one thing that Forbie hated the sight of it was tufts of straw and dung sticking up over the ploughing, and for this reason he liked to see it well spread, 'small as mice' feet', as the saying goes, so that the plough-tail could topple it into the furrow, buried from sight, humus and manure for next season's crops, breaking up and decomposing itself in the services of nature reclaiming her own. But there wasn't a tuft of sharn to be seen on Badgie's rigs, not even on the midses or shallow feerings, the seams where the ploughrigs are joined together, so that Forbie's profits from his cattle beasts was well hidden. But he wouldn't hear of you spreading the dung with a fork, which was lighter and easier on your back, with three or four sharp prongs that pierced the dung heaps easily, except when there had been a spell of frost, when you could scarcely mark the muck heaps with a shoulder pick. The first time Forbie saw you spreading dung with a fork he sent you home for a short handled byre graip, which made a better job he said, and wondered what you had learned at your last place. So you just humoured the old man and did what you was told, and apparently he was pleased with the result, your praises now ringing in Badgie's ears while he strode beside him at the plough.

Forbie liked to get a young man so that he could 'mould him to his wyes', as he told Badgie. The trouble was that the young lads never stayed long enough about the place to be 'moulded', but were up and away at the next May Term, twelve months being about the limit of their endurance of Forbie's 'auld farrant wyes o' doin' things', so that Forbie's purpose was continually being thwarted and the moulds wasted before the molten metal had solidified and taken shape to his satisfaction. So Forbie was forever casting new moulds for a cattleman to please him, and year in year out Badgie had a new neighbour next door to him at the cottar house. If you could stay for just two years as cattleman you was likely to break the record at Kingask, but really there were times when the old man tried your patience.

The only mould that had ever set to please Forbie Tait was the one he had cast for his foreman, Badgie Summers, who had been with him now for sixteen years, first at Langstraik and now twelve years at Kingask, and Forbie had so moulded Badgie that he couldn't put a foot in the wrong place; knew every move that the old man would make, and what would please him and what would not – in fact you could add that old Forbie had wound Badgie round his little finger and made him a farmer's man in every sense of the word. When the Term time came round feeing Badgie was only a formality, and when Forbie asked him to bide on for another year Badgie wouldn't say yea or nae the first time, usually waiting or Forbie tried him a second time, when Badgie would ask for an extra pound or two to his yearly wage, which mostly he got; or if the general trend was falling wages Badgie would hum and haw until Forbie agreed not to take him down in pay. So while others came and went for miles around Badgie stayed on year after year, secure in his job as foreman at Kingask, with a new stockman next door to him every second year or so, sometimes only a twelvemonth if the new billy didn't suit old Forbie.

But now it looked as though you was going to stay longer than most with Forbie Tait, and more than a year next door to Badgie Summers, and at the end of your first year you was asked to bide on in good time before the cottar market, to make sure you didn't take a fancy to moving, and you got £2 more to your wage over the next year. Even your bad hoeing had been over-looked in view of your good husbandry in the byres. In all conscience you was really a tidy hoer and next year you would be wary of the charlock weed.

But you had gone to the cottar market just the same, just to get the day off and maybe to meet some of your old cronies from the Bogside. You had come home early with the train, and after dinner, still in your marriage suit, you went a round or two with Badgie at the plough, telling him all the news of the market, the lads you had seen and where they were moving to, the things that interested Badgie, seeing you was so well in with him and settling in fine for a cottar life on the farms. About a quarter to four in the afternoon Badgie loosened his theets from the swingletrees and hooped them on the backbands of his pair and went down the brae to sort your nowt, past the cottar houses, sitting on Jug's back, the chains swinging by her sides under Badgie's tackety boots. After tea you was off to the pictures in Brochan, off to see Constance Bennett in *Topper*, with Roland Young; not by choice but because they had closed one of the picture houses and there was nothing else to see. This was another side of your life that Badgie nor anyone else could understand; except that you was 'picture daft', and any arty side of the business never entered their heads.

It was in the early summer of your second year at Kingask that you made your first real effort in journalism. Here for the first time in your strange incongruous life you was going to see yourself in print. You had been writing when you was at the school, and again when you was off work for a month when you was single, living with your parents after an attack of epilepsy. But these efforts never emerged from longhand, silly childish stories from the brain and hand of a schoolboy. This time you were to flourish in bold type in Forbie's daily paper. Of course you didn't know this yet and as it turned out to be abortive in relation to the rest of your career it wasn't all that important. But it was a start, a faint glimmer of the light that was to shine so brightly for you in much later years. It was so transient at this stage that dear Kathleen scarcely noticed it, though it did seem strange for her that her man should get a letter in the newspapers: a half column on the ethics of the bill newly introduced by Parliament to bring unemployment benefit to the farm workers. It was perhaps your one and only venture on the political spectrum and fair amazed the folk next door and the neighbours for miles around. To think that they lived next door to a cheil who got letters printed in the papers fair amazed them, and when a second epistle was printed they just couldn't get over it and you was the talk of the turnip fields for weeks on end.

Of course old Forbie had read your letters but made no comment about them; maybe thinking you was a bit touched in the head and would soon be standing for Parliament, in which case he would have to look for another cattleman, maybe one who didn't have his head so much in the clouds above the cottar house on the brae at Kingask. What was more important was that Forbie's daughter had read your letters in the press, especially Deborah, who (to your surprise) was herself something of a freelance journalist and had her weekly spot in a farming journal. She sought to encourage you and gave you books to read: *Blood Relations*, by Sir Phillip Gibbs, and a translation from the French on *The Life of Napoleon*. You became newspaper daft and read every article you could lay eyes on, mostly from Forbie's *Press & Journal*, which was a day old before you got it from Badgie, or Beaverbrook's *Daily Express*, which you could get in the village for a penny; two-pence for the weekly *Illustrated*, and fourpence for *Picture Post*, also the Sunday papers you could afford and your film weeklies, one or two of which you had read from boyhood. It was all grist for the mill and you just couldn't get enough of the stuff to keep you going, even though you worked a ten-hour-day six days a week and Sundays once a fortnight and had only the evenings to spare. To be in love with something like this is an experience you wouldn't like to have missed: this inner fire that burns you up with a delightful glow and devours slothful time with relish, bringing you alive to the fingertips. Strange that this hunger for the printed word should come upon you now – you that had been born and brought up in a home where not a book existed, scarcely even a bible; everything you had read had been borrowed or loaned, except for the occasional twopenny Comic Cuts or Comic Chips or the fourpenny Buffalo Bill novel, Sexton Blake or Dixon Hawke you had picked up at the bookstalls. Even yet, in the second year of your marriage there wasn't a book in the house longer than you had taken to read it, then returned to the source from which you had borrowed it.

But now you felt you had read enough to be able to write an article, even two articles; so with writing fire in your brain and red ink in your veins you set off on your bike to Brochan for foolscap (fool's cap – and now you know why they call it that) ink and pen-nibs, then sat down in all earnestness to write a fruitless essay for newsprint. Of course it was hopeless, even before you started, being in longhand for one thing. But you enclosed a spare envelope with stamp in case of rejection and waited, guarding your secret closely and telling Kathleen not to mention it to Mrs Summers, because Badgie and young Tom would likely laugh at you in the stable if they heard of such a thing. But just wait till they saw your name heading an article in the daily paper; not a letter mind you, but a full-grown article you would get paid for, then you could afford to let them laugh – all of them, old Forbie among them, laugh their fill. Maybe you had deceived yourself too long with the idea that you was meant to be a farm worker, while all the time you was a born journalist with ink in your veins – or so you deluded yourself; and now you found yourself on a road with no turning. Maybe the craze for cold print would ease off but in the meantime it burned with incandescent brilliance and brightened your dull skies for weeks on end.

The article came back with your first rejection slip, the first of nearly a hundred that were to follow, but as you were not aware of the prospect it didn't dampen the flame that burned within you; on the contrary the setback merely inspired you to write still further, another article; this time confiding in Deborah, the farmer's daughter, and she revised your work. It was a sort of documentary on the evolution or development in shipbuilding, particularly in Scotland, from the primitive hewn out tree-trunks of the early Picts to the launching of the Queen Mary on the Clyde, with most other things in between, from the Roman and Viking galleys to the Wooden Walls, China Clippers, Windjammers, the Comet, and paddle to screw-driven steamships. The idea had come to you from a picture on a calendar hanging in your mother's kitchen, depicting two cavemen in animal skins hacking out their boat from a fallen tree-trunk with their stone axes, tied to the shafts with hide thongs – an idea that kindled your imagination on how far shipbuilding had progressed from this primitive beginning to the Mighty *Queen Mary*. The boat-building yard at Candlebay had also coloured your mind, besides your present nearness to the sea and passing ships; even battleships like the *Hood, Nelson* and *Rodney,* on their way from Rosyth to Scapa Flow, and you had started smoking Senior Service cigarettes to get pictures of the great Dreadnoughts. Your last article had been about the little fishing village of Spitullie along the coast and maybe it had little appeal for publication. This was a much wider canvas and with Deborah's revision you was convinced of acceptance, even in longhand – such are the vain hopes of the devoted scribe.

Of course you failed again and this your first real fling at journalism died the natural death it deserved. And never again did you ever ask anyone to revise your work. And what did you want to be a journalist for anyway? Surely you had seen enough of newspaper movies to show you the rat race it really was: American talkies like *Front Page*, *Scandal Sheet* and *Hi Nellie*, seen in your single days and not yet forgotten. First you had wanted to be a film projectionist; mad about the job you was but never got a start. And here you was cottared now with a wife and bairn and still mucking out byres and feeding nowt and dreaming about this never never world that still eluded you from afar off. You didn't realize it then but you were actually on the threshold of a venture that was going to cost you forty years of struggle and frustration and heartbreak before the final joy of achievement. Now you have reached that goal you can look back with pride on your perseverance against all odds, with all the doors slammed in your face; with no education, no influence, no backing, no money, nothing but bare fisted determination, yet with these handicaps you had literally battered down editors' doors and had their readers look at your hack – even beyond the first paragraph, right to the end, and then it reached the editor's desk. Eventually you had them print the stuff, in full detail, not a comma changed or an exclamation mark – though spelling wasn't so good. When you read the galley proofs it was the greatest thrill of your life; like a young mother with her first baby . . . something else you wouldn't have missed for all the tears it cost you.

And now you can tell the world about these two men and their boat; those cavemen in their animal skins with their thonged axes, hulling out their canoe from a fallen tree . . . you can tell it after forty years of crying in the wilderness, and people can read about the inspiration for one of your very first unpublished articles; an article that never saw the light and couldn't be reconstructed because you have forgotten the details.

But old Forbie Tait never lived to see your success. 'The mere fact o' being alive killed him in time,' just as he had said, and he was gathered at last with his brother farmers in the kirkyard at Peatriggs. But you knew what his comment would have been at the stable sessions in the evenings at Kingask, had he lived to see

154

his old stockman in book form: 'By gum, them that lives langest sees the maist ferlies!'

Badgie Summers wasn't long after you at Kingask either, only two more years. When Forbie asked him to bide on the first time Badgie said he hadn't made up his mind, but Forbie didn't give him the usual second chance, and that was the end of Badgie at Kingask.

Glossary of Scots words

Airt area, direction

Bailie cattleman or water-bailie, and can also apply to bailiff or municipal magistrate in Scotland
Bawbees money
Beuk book
Bicker a dish
Bide stay, wait
Bing heap
Birse temper, anger
Blibber dribble, trickle
Braw grand, bright, gaudy
Breeks breeches, trousers
Breet opposite of brute; one deserving sympathy
Bubblie Jock, turkey – cock
Bucht shed, wooden building or lean-to

Canny careful, to avoid risk, slow
Canty cheery
Causey causey stones: floor or yard laid with cobblestones
Chap to chap, to knock, a blow; to mash potatoes — Noun: a fellow
Chaumer sleeping quarters for single farm workers
Chauve struggle, fight
Cheil man; also spelt *chiel*
Clacht to clutch, grasp, hold
Claes clothes, dress, apparel
Claik gossip
Clart smear
Cloo ball of wool or straw
Clyack clyack sheaf: the last bound sheaf of the harvest
Cornkist large wooden chest for holding corn
Cottar married farmworker in tied cottage
Crabbit crusty, short tempered

Dab-hand good at his job; good with his hands
Dachle to hesitate; go slow
Darg dig; daily-drag: daily routine
Dirl to ring, shrill, vibration
Divot sod, turf
Dother daughter
Dottled in dotage: absent-minded
Drizzen dull, colourless, cheerless
Dumfoonert dumbfounded, confounded, struck dumb

Fash fuss
Fee or **Fee-ed** to employ, engaged for work
Fleer floor
Foon foundation
Foonert foundered, to sink down
Forrard forward
Fraiky friendly, to placate; to pet, pettish
Fule dirty, soiled
Fusker moustache, whiskers

Gear, Geir goods, riches, possessions
Geet, Geat a child, plural: geets
Gelding young castrated horse
Genteel gentle, refined, cultured
Gig small horse cart or car, mostly with solid rubber tyres
Glaur mud, slime, mess
Glory-hole hiding place, concealment
Gouk fool, idiot; playing the fool
Grat cried, wept. Past tense of greet
Greep floor of byre or stable
Greet to cry, weep
Grieve foreman in charge, gaffer
Grubber heavy cultivator

Hairst harvest
Halflin young man; male teenager
Hanker longing, desire, craving
Hantle numerous, a great many
Hippens baby nappies
Hirple to limp, limping, cripple
Hurdies hips
Hyowe hoe
Hyter to swagger

157

Ill-faured ill-featured, ugly

Kittle to brighten up, spirited
Kittlin' kitten; verb: kittlin'
Knowe brae, mound, summit

Lade millrace
Lair peat moss
Leer liar; one who tells lies
Limmer girl of loose moral behaviour; mischievous
Loon boy
Loup to leap
Lour to darken, cloudy
Lugs ears
Lum chimney

Mair more
Mastitis udder infection
Moggan money-bag, sock or stocking, sometimes spats or leggings
Muckle quantity, large
Muffler scarf or large 'kerchief worn round the throat

Neist next
New-fangled up-to-date, unorthodox, new invention
Nowt cattle, oxen

Orraman odd job man
Oxter arm-pit, breast

Pap teat, female breast
Perquisites provisions in lieu of wages, a form of barter, probably of
   Feudal origin
Phaeton four-wheeled horse vehicle
Pickiesae soft tweed hat
Piece sandwich lunch
Pleiter wet muddy conditions; working in the rain
Pleuch plough
Plough stilts plough handles
Pooch pocket
Puckle quantity
Pucklie small quantity

Quine girl

Randie bitch, a cheat; loose living
Rape rope. Rope of straw or sprotts
Rax to stretch
Ripe to rifle, rob; to take by force
Rive to tear, wrench
Roup auction sale
Rouse to anger
Ruck cornstock, sometimes rick
Runt stem, stalk; kale runt

Sark shirt
Scrach to cry out like a hen; to scraich
Screich screech
Scunner disgust; to be put off
Segs reeds, rushes, water-grass
Sharn cow dung
Shelt pony, small horses
Shied to take fright; to waver, to shy away
Sic such
Siller money, sterling silver
Skeelie skilful
Skirl scream
Skite small quantity; to skid
Smiler small rake, pulled by rope from the shoulder
Sort to repair, to attend to; to tend the cattle
Speir to ask, to enquire
Spruce tidy, neat, clean
Spunk spark, tinder
Stamagaster shock, surprise
Steer bullock, also stir; to stir up, commotion
Stickit-nieve clenched fist
Stite nonsense
Stock or **Stoke** same as breet; unfortunate man
Stot castrated bullock or male ox
Straik to stroke, to whet a scythe with broadstraik
Stramash tumult, confusion
Stravaigin' to wander, travel
Stroop Spout, penis
Strushle rough, untidy, shabby
Styter stagger, stumbling; unsteady on his feet
Surtoo Surtout coat, mostly black; frockcoat
Swack swift; also swuppert, meaning fast, quick

Teem empty

Tether leash, chain, fetters; life-span

Thacket-biggin' cottage with thatched roof

Thocht thought, imagination

Thrapple throat, neck

Thraw-heuk winding hook for straw rapes or making ropes with sisal twine

Thrawn stubborn

Timmer timber

Toshle tassle

Track or **Traikit** disorderly, untidy, shabbily dressed

Trauchle travail, struggle, hard-labour

Trig tidy, firm

Troch or **Trochie** small wooden trough

Wall-tams or **Nicky-tams** leather straps with buckles worn under the knees by workmen, especially farmworkers

Wark work

Warsle wrestle

Wheeble whistle, piping call of the curlew

Yark or **Dunt** to rap, knock; a blow

Yavel second year in crop

Yird earth, ground

Yoke wooden spar for pulling plough

Yoking time time for starting work

Yowl shout, to cry out, howl